The White Lodge

Others by Peter Telemark:

The Valley of the Night
Wulfsdgerd
(part of The Berserkr of Borealea series)

The Witch of Death Swamp
The House of Dust
The Cellar in Ghost Hill
The Eighth Otter
The Footprints in the Winter Woods
The Timber-Witch of the Mountain Forest
The Habitants of Murdering-Town
The Werewolf of Deadham
(part of the Seth Athenor series)

For further information about the author/other books,
please visit our website:

Petertelemarkbooks.com

For my Eva

THE WHITE LODGE

By

Peter Telemark

There is an ancient lodge in the winter woods,

    Built of white, cracked, and crumbling stone

    That stands amid the pallid trees, silent and alone,

But inside, something malign waits, listens, and broods.

No traveler comes to stay there anymore.

    But they say that many years ago,

    When the blizzards would gust and blow,

Grateful wayfarers would rap upon its door.

The last echoes of their knock would dwindle and die but

    No answer would come from inside to their calls.

    Baffled, they would open the unlocked door,

    And enter to find only debris on the dusty floor.

    Then, something pale slowly emerged from the walls,

And behind, with finality, the sentient door closed shut.

— The Legend of the White Lodge

PROLOGUE

"Travel not alone when the snows come to Loreley Town."

The words still echoed in Chetwynd Pym's thoughts as he trudged along the snow-carpeted road. They had been spoken by a traveling tinker at the Tatzelwürm Rathskeller with whom he had been drinking in town. The man did not coin the phrase but was merely quoting a local legend. The fellow was a shabby, half-besotted ragamuffin who had pointed his tankard at him, ale slopping over onto their table, as he made that cryptic remark.

The man, who named himself Kikkert, was a stranger to him. The Dutch surname translated to "Frog," and he did somewhat resemble one, with a broad, jowly face and a tongue forever darting out to lick his pendulous lips. Being wary, Pym had refused his offer to accompany him and considered the warning to be either a ploy to encourage his company or merely drunken nattering.

It was a long way from Philadelphia to Droitwijk Town in New York Province. But Pym had a wandering foot, one that had recently taken him from New York City to Pennsylvania Province. In addition, his was a solitary nature, reinforced by the disdain and mockery he so often met in his travels. Even as a child, his peers used to jeer at him for his lack of wits, calling him "Cretin" Pym.

Later, in symbolic refutation, he had an owl tattooed on his arm, reflecting the popular belief that this bird was wise. Only to be told some years afterward by a knowledgeable hunter that owls were among the stupidest of birds, less trainable than even crows.

Perhaps it was understandable why his life became what it was.

But he was getting older, and arthritis had increasingly started to trouble him. He had a sister living in Droitwijk, in the *Lucht Eland* or "Sky Elk" River Valley, who would take him in. He dreamed of warming himself at her hearth and finally settling down to what years remained to him.

Had he any money, he could have returned to New York City, booked passage up the Hudson River to Albany, and cut across to Droitwijk, a mere fifty miles due west. But he had none and was forced to travel overland north more than 200 miles toward Droitwijk. At least there were well-traveled roads in-between, including the one he now traversed – *Die Hopfenkrötenstraße* or "The Hop-Toad Road." That was the translation of the older Lenape name *Kaxkxàkës Métëme*, presumably referring to a one-time proliferation of the reptiles, although few were seen anymore. The road originated in the center of Loreley Town, the county seat of Pastorius County in northeastern Pennsylvania Province, and threaded north to end at the border with New York Province.

But, starting from Philadelphia in late October 1754 as he had, he only made it as far as Loreley, where he had been forced to wait out the winter, relying on the charity of the local Lutheran church for food and shelter.

But his use of alms to support a drinking habit had not endeared him to the Lutheran pastor, Oreste von Mardure, who finally reached his limit when in a drunken stupor, Pym had impulsively pulled down his pants, squatted and defecated in the aisle of the church nave. The few congregants seated there in silent prayer were understandably aghast and not shy about making their revulsion known to Von Mardure.

The pastor was a grumpy but kind man but had no choice. Pym found himself wandering the streets of Loreley Town, begging for food and coin. Realizing he had to leave the city, winter or not, Pym set out north in January 1755.

He heard there was a friendly Christian Lenape village in the foothills of the nearby mountains that might shelter him. There, if he was lucky, he could wait out the snows until it was safe to travel north into New York Province. He was told there was another friendly village – this one of the Iroquois, called *Ochenang* – just across the border. From there it was about 100 miles northeastward to Droitwijk.

But he needed shelter in the meantime. The Lenape village was about ten miles north of Loreley Town, and in between was a tree-dotted plain and scattered thickets and woods. It was now late afternoon, and snow had started to fall, driven by a bitter wind that slashed through his moth-eaten bearskin coat.

He had met a group of hunters on horseback, a deer carcass draped over one horse, on their way back to town. They had eyed him suspiciously and refused to return his tentative greeting. As they passed him, one turned around to gaze at him, and for a moment he thought to see pity in that face. Then, the man turned his back and followed the rest of the hunters down the winding road until they all vanished in the snowfall.

He glanced about him worriedly. He could see the forested foothills a few miles ahead, the white trees mantling up to the snow-tipped eastern mountains. There he would find the Lenape village – *Kùmhòkunk*, they called it, meaning "In the Clouds," although to the residents of Loreley, *Wolkendorf* or "Cloud Village" was preferable.

Squinting ahead up the road, he made out a side trail leading east. That was curious. With the snow several feet deep, he could not understand why the side road seemed marked so plainly. As he trudged nearer, he saw that it was a narrow channel, almost as if someone had shoveled it out recently, piling snow along its edges.

He paused to cudgel his memory. He seemed to recall overhearing someone mention that path, and that it led to a ruined house or tavern in the woods. Later, when he asked some congregants at church about it, they became furtive and unresponsive.

He shrugged away his disquietude and turned onto the path, while the wind swirled snowflakes about his hunched shoulders. He plodded along mechanically and did not look up from the trail. At length, the wind died away, and the snowfall tapered off as he neared the edge of the trees.

A churning sound made him pause to glance back. The sky was an overarching gray with patches of lurid white. But now, about a mile or so to the west, one of the low-hanging gray clouds seemed to dip, and slowly a spiral began whirling up from the snowy ground. It seemed like a column of ashen smoke, and he could see it link with the clouds and then begin to slowly twist across the terrain.

It was not the first snow tornado he had seen, and he watched with interest for a moment. He knew that – unlike tornados in the other seasons – winter tornados invariably spun slowly and were barely capable of inflicting any destruction.

He was about to turn back when he saw additional movement in front of the tornado. It looked like six more tornados, but they were small, each perhaps the size of a man. He searched in vain for any tether to the clouds. If it had been summer, he would have thought them harmless dust devils. But these…

At first, they seemed to whirl frantically away from the larger tornado. Then, when they had gained some distance from it, they all simultaneously paused to hover, in a way no whirlwinds ever did. Pym goggled at them with bewilderment as they gathered into a circle, and realized with mounting dread that they were no mere manifestation of nature.

They were living beings.

Even as he tried to wrap his mind around that, the vortexes all began to move in his direction, as if they had sensed his presence in some way. As they purposefully assembled into a V-shaped formation and began to converge toward him, he let out a cry and took to his heels down the path.

Now, amid the white silence, he thought to hear fierce whispers behind him – not only the whisper of whirling wind but the whisper of unearthly voices talking to each other in some unguessable tongue.

Terrified, Pym turned and started running down the path into the woods. Here, the trail continued, winding through the trees, which had spared it from much snow. He was able to make quick progress, ducking beneath low snow-laden boughs and around slight bends.

He once glanced back, and it was all he could do to stifle a scream. For, behind him, one after the other in a line, came the whispering vortexes, pursuing him. Fragments of their wordless murmurs and mutters preceded them, melding and swelling like the thunder of a gathering storm.

Pym broke into a sprint, his breath coming in gasps, lifting his legs high. The trees flanking him began to thin out and he suddenly debouched into a small glade, encircled by tall, snowy pine and beech. He staggered and almost fell.

He was expecting ruins, perhaps a crumbled foundation and part of a chimney. Instead, there stood a house that seemed almost new, with lattice-paned windows at both stories and a solid-looking front door that was slightly ajar. The house was colored all white, and as he resumed his flight, he saw it was built of stone, even to the flat roof and the cupola perched atop its right side. Not daring to look back, he raced to the door, shoved it open, and plunged inside, slamming it behind and latching it. There was neither bolt nor bar, and he desperately cast about for something to block it.

He was in a large, rectangular chamber, with a dead hearth taking up one wall and various pieces of broken furniture strewn about. There was a long table lying on its side, sagging and splintered, and several armchairs whose faded fabric clung in tatters. An armoire still stood upright against a wall, although its glass doors were cracked and shattered. The floor was of dark wood, warped and riven in places.

Much of the room was swathed in darkness, especially the debris-crowded corners.

Had he a lantern or candle to inspect those corners, he might have seen scattered white fragments of what had once been human skeletal remains.

But he had no time to wonder at the contrast between the immaculate outside and the debris-strewn inside. He rushed to the table and frantically dragged it across the uneven floor and shoved it up against the door. Just as he did, the door rattled f iercely, and he leaped back as the table was savagely flung aside. He watched as the door violently shuddered, and puffs of snow spurted through its chinks. But it held and he stumbled back with a sigh of relief.

He heard something brushing against the door, like the sound of many swirling brooms. Then, the brushing noises parted to left and right and scoured the walls flanking the door. There was a slithering scratching across one latticed window and then at the next. Pym glanced at the dark diamond panes but could see nothing. By degrees, the sounds died away and an oppressive silence fell.

It took many minutes for Pym to recover himself enough to survey the room. There was a chandelier, with some candle-nubs remaining. But he had no flint and steel to strike flame or to build a fire in the hearth. An open doorway led to the kitchen, where more half-spent candles were scattered across the counters. The kitchen had a small fireplace, which he suspected joined the sitting room hearth in a common chimney f ue. The hinged lid to the larder stood open but he found nothing inside it but dust.

He stopped for a moment to notice that there was no sign of rat or mice pellets, no spiderwebs, no sign that any pest had ever been there. That was curious since even a vacant house might provide a home for such vermin. He returned to the sitting room and made his way to a second doorway that led to a recess where a curving stairway climbed. Like all else, it was fashioned of pallid stone.

He marveled at that, since in that part of Pennsylvania, stone was not easily quarried, and was usually reserved for foundations and chimneys in otherwise wooden houses. But he had no guess why this house had been built here at all. Perhaps it was once a lodge for travelers on Hop-Toad Road, long since fallen into disuse. But why?

He mounted to the second-floor back hallway, where a series of three doors fronted a line of windows. The windows were like those on the first floor, diamond-paned and opaque. The floor in the hallway was also of some dark wood, but better preserved than in the sitting room.

He selected the first door and entered to find himself in a spacious chamber with a cold hearth along one wall. The windows threw the last remnants of daylight into the room. To his surprise, the furnishings were not decayed or disarrayed. There was a large, four-poster bed without a canopy. It had no sheets or blankets, and a moment's inspection of the sagging mattress found it stuffed with dried and rancid straw. Yet, the two armchairs flanking the fireplace still seemed intact, although their linen coverings had rotted away.

Curiosity overcoming his apprehension, he returned to the hallway and entered the second room. He stared around it with amazement. All was intact here as well. It appeared to be some kind of library, the walls lined with bookshelves and a large desk with a chair. Another candelabra hung low, some of its sockets still fixed with unlit candles. There was no hearth in this room, perhaps why it was chosen for a library, to protect against accidental fire.

On the desk were a long-evaporated inkwell and a quill pen. There were sheets of parchment strewn across the desk, covered with indecipherable symbols. A few iron-bound books lay nearby, one of which was opened to pages with minuscule letters in Latin. Meager as Pym's education had been, he could recognize that language when he saw it, although could not read a single word of it.

Baffled, he left the room and went to the final chamber. From inside, he thought he heard a whisper – not like the ones he had heard outside, but more like someone quietly weeping. He hesitated at the door, feeling a palpable apprehension, then edged it open. Unlike the first two, this one had no windows of its own. The only light trickled in from the windows in the hallway.

He could not see much of anything and perhaps it was a trick of the light, but he thought the brown wallpaper rippled and for just an instant it looked like reddish skin or hide. He blinked and wiped his eyes, and when he looked again, the wallpaper was as he first glimpsed it.

His eyes fell upon a curious pedestal in the center of the room. Upon it was what seemed to be a statue of an animal skull. Pym could not tell what kind of animal – it might have been a huge bird, with that long beak. But what bird had rows of sharp teeth with two long fore-fangs in the upper jaw? It might have been an alligator or similar reptile, he thought. Between the two hollow orbits, there was a third hole, this one rectangular rather than circular. He approached and gingerly touched it, running his finger around the rim, finding it smooth. He craned his head to inspect the rear of it and noted the neat severance of the fossilized spine.

Shrinking back from the pedestal uneasily, he hurried back out and closed the door. As the last ray of light left the room, something in the far corner was briefly visible, had Pym remained long enough to look.

It was the arm of an ebony throne, and lying limply along it was the skeletal hand of what had once been a man – or something similar to a man. A long brown robe shrouded the sitting figure and from the hem protruded a skeletal lower limb. But it was not a foot. It was a hoof.

In the hallway, he idly glanced at the far end, where an iron spiral staircase twisted up to a trapdoor in the ceiling, presumably leading to the cupola atop the roof.

He returned to the first room and shut the door behind him. It, too, had no bolt or bar, but the latch seemed firm enough. He set down his pack and cautiously stretched out on the bed. He nodded to himself. This room seemed suitable for spending the night. Hopefully, with the dawn, those…those things…might be gone. What a fool he was to have traveled alone! He should have taken the nattering ragamuffin at the rathskeller seriously.

As he drifted into sleep, there came a soft susurration, like a breath of wind blowing down the chimney into the dark and cold hearth.

1. Farewell to Leichtenberg

By April, snow had given way to rain in the town of
Leichtenberg on the Spirit River. Here, in the upcountry
of His Majesty's Province of New York, the weather was
generally miserable except for the brief mercy of the summer.
On this day, hail clattered on the steeply gabled roofs like a
nest of striking rattlesnakes.

Seth Athenor took one last look out the second-story
French windows. In the plaza below, he could see a few
unlucky townsfolk scurrying to their homes, heads ducked
and cloaks whipping about their legs in the downpour. To
the north, dark clouds with intermittent flashes of lightning
churned above the peaks of the forested Spirit Mountains.
Even though it was only a little past noon, it seemed as dark
as night.

He was remembering what had happened in December
1754 – how Dereham Mayor Ulysse von Mardure had come
in answer to an urgent plea from his brother Laerte and had
asked Athenor to come along. Accompanying them had
been Lieutenant Rodrigo Archer, tasked by British Army
Command to assess the situation in the area, what with the
start of hostilities between the British and the French earlier
that year.

They had not encountered any menace from the French
or their Indian allies. It was something infinitely worse – a
horde of vampire-ghosts that had scampered across the
rooftops and left a trail of bloodless bodies behind. In the
end, they managed to defeat those hellacious creatures in

time for grateful Christmas celebrations, and since then, the townsfolk feted them as heroes.[1]

But with the restoration of peace, unwelcome changes came to Leichtenberg. Laerte, who had suspended his tenure as magistrate judge to serve as *pro tem* mayor, found himself ejected from that role. One of the leading merchants of Leichtenberg, Lars Schninkner, and his allies gathered enough support for him to replace Laerte. The rationale was that the town needed Laerte to resume his judgeship more than it needed him as mayor.

Although he recognized the merits of that argument, Laerte was nonetheless bitter. He felt that he had shepherded the town through a terrible period and had been unceremoniously cast aside regardless. In addition, he had enjoyed being the temporary *Bürgermeister* and had hoped the Council would make it permanent.

Ironically, Ulysse had lately been wishing he were a judge instead of a mayor, and now it seemed his prayers were answered – partly. The previous month, he had received a letter from the Town Council in Dereham. During his absence, Gordon Riley, the owner of the local Gray Owl Inn, had served as what was supposed to be his temporary replacement. But either by dint of extraordinary competence (which Ulysse doubted) or chicanery (more likely), the Council voted to make his mayorship permanent.

Unlike his brother, Ulysse greeted the news with relief. He had been Dereham's mayor for only a couple of years, having previously practiced law in the neighboring town of

---

[1] As related in *The Habitants of Murdering-Town*

Droitwijk. The Council that now replaced him was the
same one that had originally begged him to take the position.

But he had always hated the job — it seemed to him
more a matter of mollifying the ambitions, quarrels, and
petty rivalries of the Council than serving the public good.
So, upon the news, he shed no tears but sent a petition
to the Royal Governor of New York Province to ask for
an appointment as the magistrate judge in Dereham. The
position had been "vacated" rather abruptly by the previous
magistrate judge, Benedict Fletcher, who had been slain by
a supernatural creature (one that Athenor himself finally
killed).[2] However, his appointment was not a sure thing,
he realized, since he was aware that the governor had a pet
crony also being considered for the job — Leigh Kynaston,
who was not even a lawyer.[3] It was remarked that Kynaston's
chief talent was being a "fart-catcher" of the governor and
that his education was so meager that he was unable to write
three consecutive sentences in correct English.

On this stormy afternoon, the brothers, Lieutenant
Archer, and Athenor had gathered one last time in Laerte's
commodious house, in the second-floor study, to exchange
their farewells.

Athenor let the maroon curtain slide back across the
French windows and turned to the study. Floor-to-ceiling
bookcases lined two walls, a third was taken up by a broad
hearth from which a crackling fire threw welcome heat.

---

[2] As related in *The Eighth Otter*

[3] Judgeships were open to non-lawyers throughout the 18th century in
both British America and America.

Floor lamps with multi-candled fixtures shed light onto the armchairs, where two of the men were seated.

One of them, Archer, was a burly man with a greying black beard, dressed in the crimson uniform of a British officer. The other was Ulysse, a small man with a sallow face. Reading glasses were perched on his long nose as he perused a book.

Another brace of candles sat atop the large desk where a middle-aged man with iron hair and a Van Dyke beard was sipping a glass of Riesling. He turned as Athenor came near and cocked a sardonic eyebrow.

"Doctor, I think you'll find that checking the storm every few minutes will not make it abate."

The man he addressed was six feet in height, with dark hair that had started to recede into a widow's peak, a hawk-like nose, and a habitually grim mouth that now twitched with a slight smile.

"I crave your pardon, Laerte. I tend to chafe at enforced inactivity."

"He can't pardon you," Ulysse rasped. "You'd have to ask the governor."

Archer chuckled. "Why, I do think you're developing a sense of humor, Ulysse."

"It's either that or go mad, Rodrigo." Ulysse permitted himself a smile. "We've been in town since November, and it's only now that the ice floes have broken up on the river. Not as though any of us will be sailing home to Dereham, it seems."

"Yes, very amusing, brother," Laerte von Mardure scowled, then returned to Athenor. "And, Doctor, I'll remind you for the thousandth time to please refer to me only as 'Judge,' and not use my forename."

"Even after all we've been through together?" Athenor tried to mute his sarcasm.

Laerte set his wine glass down and pursed his lips. "You know I'm grateful to you and Lieutenant Archer for what you've done here these last few months. Not just against that horde of vampires, but the medical care you've provided to our citizens."

"What?" Ulysse interrupted mockingly. "You don't think those citizens miss the tender treatments of Dr. Schweibel?" Auguste Schweibel was a longstanding physician in town and had some basic competence, so long as he remained sober – which was infrequent.

"Oh, you mean treatment with liquor?" Archer barked out a laugh. "He not only drinks it. It's the only medicine he seems to prescribe."

Laerte glowered at him, irritated by the interruptions. He turned back to Athenor. "As I was saying, Doctor. You've done quite a lot, especially for those poor ironworkers at the Schoepflin Foundry."

"It was but a simple suggestion," Athenor demurred. "To put cloths over their nose and mouth when working. So, they wouldn't inhale so much metal dust particles and gradually sicken."

"No one seems to have connected their sickness with fumes from the blast furnace until you." Laerte gave him a grudging smile.

Athenor shifted with embarrassment. "It's not the first time I've seen 'metal fume fever.' I'm just pleased I was of help."

"At least the foundry's new owner didn't object." Laerte scowled. "That's something intelligent Lars Schninkner has done for once in his useless life."

Ulysse set his book aside. "We quite understand, brother. I'm sure it wasn't easy to give up being the *pro tem Bürgermeister* and return to your judgeship. But I'd think you would be happy to rid yourself of that thankless office."

"But to have the Council elect that fat imbecile Schninkner, of all people!" Laerte slapped his hand down on the desk. "What does a merchant – a farmer, an absentee landlord, a thrice-damned publican – know about running a government?"

"That imbecile has many powerful friends," Ulysse replied. "Many of them in the Merchant Guild have dual membership in the Town Council. Why would they prefer a principled mayor over one that promotes their interests?"

Laerte had no answer but snatched up a bell sitting at his elbow and rang it. "Where is that dratted butler? He was supposed to serve supper an hour ago."

"Adolphus?" Archer grinned. "Maybe it's taken him extra time to finish spitting in our food."

Laerte glanced at the lieutenant sourly. "I don't know why all of you seem to detest him. He gives me good service."

"Perhaps because he makes a corpse seem festive by comparison," Athenor suggested. "In fact, I once suspected he might be one of the vampires himself."

Laerte grunted. "At least he doesn't keep chattering on and on…like some people." His squinted gaze swept them all.

Just then, there was a rap at the door to the study and the supercilious butler entered, serving tray in his hands. He walked stiffly to the low tabouret in the middle of the room and set it down. He did not look at any of the occupants, much less address them. He merely glanced at Laerte for any further instruction and when the judge waved a dismissive hand, marched sullenly out, closing the door behind him.

"Ah," Archer rose, approached the table, and smacked his lips. "What do we have here?'

Ulysse and Laerte both got up and joined him, while Athenor did not move. The judge inspected the food and nodded his satisfaction.

"Hmm, beer, bratwurst, boiled potatoes, green beans, and…quark pudding." He helped himself to one of the stacked plates and began ladling food onto it. Ulysse and Archer followed his example and returned to their chairs, along with tankards of beer that they set on side tables.

Finally, Athenor filled his plate, disdaining the green beans, and found a chair next to the desk. Setting the plate atop it, he crossed himself and bowed his head briefly.

Laerte had just finished a forkful of potatoes and froze with embarrassment, then hastily crossed himself and continued eating. Ulysse caught the gesture out of the corner of his eye and hurriedly imitated it, while Archer just shrugged and forked a piece of sausage into his mouth.

While quite knowledgeable about Scripture, the lieutenant was a desultory Anglican, having long ago been estranged from the ministers of his church in Dereham.

They ate for a few minutes in silence, then Laerte looked up from his plate and pointed his fork at Athenor's.

"You don't care for those *gruene bohnen* – those green beans, Doctor?"

Athenor shook his head. "Much too green for my taste," he joked. Occasionally, his humor was feeble. This was one of those times.

Laerte rolled his eyes. "What about you, Lieutenant? Is all to *your* taste?"

Archer took a swig of beer. "Judge, I must have gained ten pounds in the last couple of months. It's probably good that I will be leaving tomorrow, or you would have to wheelbarrow me out of town."

Athenor turned to him, brow wrinkled with worry. "Are you sure you don't want me to accompany you?"

Archer waved a dismissive hand. "Too dangerous for a…civilian like you. This is a military assignment, as you know." He had almost said "deserter." He had known about Athenor's past for several years.

"To reconnoiter near the ruins of Fort White Pine, northwest of us in the mountains?" Laerte asked.

"Just so," Archer replied. "With the war underway, Army Command wants more information about that area."

"Surely, they could send soldiers from Fort Oswego at the southeast margin of Lake Ontar'io?" Laerte pursued.

Archer shook his head. "French and Huron spies watch that fort constantly, mapping their movements. But a small party heading up the Spirit River and then cutting north should easily evade any enemy eyes."

"But I'm very familiar with that area, as you know," Athenor sought the lieutenant's eyes.

"I do know," Archer replied, with a slight wink. "But I'll say it again – too dangerous for a civilian and especially for you. You probably have some old Huron or French enemies that still lurk there."

Athenor did not immediately reply. In 1742, he had been Ensign Sacha Athenois, a French Colonial Marine, whose commanders had sent him on a mission to assassinate the garrison at the British Fort White Pine. Ultimately, he refused to carry out that terrible assignment and had been forced to desert to the British. But the fort was destroyed regardless, by a supernatural agency. He had left it behind him, along with the nearby Abenaki village of *Lawana* – "Laughing Water," where he lost his Abenaki wife. Even after all these years, the memory still stabbed at him.[4]

---

[4] As related in *The Footprints in the Winter Woods*

"They might not be the only enemy in that vicinity," He gazed knowingly at Archer, to whom he had long since related that history. But, in the many years since then, no rumors of the creature's return had been heard. Considering its immense size, it could scarcely have gone unnoticed, even in the wilderness.

"I understand." Archer let out a slight sigh of resignation. "But I won't be alone. As you know, I'm taking Lieutenant Fergus Hyland and our three redcoat friends, Isaacs, Fox, and Moore."

"They all have frontier experience," Athenor said. "And all of them proved their worth against the vampires."[5]

"I'm sure Rodrigo will be fine," Ulysse turned to Athenor impatiently. "But he has four soldiers to go with him, while there will only be the two of us on the road south to Pennsylvania."

"As far as we know, there are no hostile tribes between here and there – just friendly Iroquois and Lenape," Athenor responded. "But I suppose one can never predict what rogue warriors or Provincial bandits prowl the roads and trails."

"Don't be too confident about the Lenape," cautioned Archer. "Some are friendly, others are still loyal to France."

"I think we can trust the Lenape village outside of Loreley Town," interjected Ulysse. "They have long been friends with the townsfolk, including Cousin Oreste."

"Yes, the Lutheran pastor you mentioned," Athenor said. "He's the one that sent you that letter by Royal Mail courier."

---

[5] As related in *The Habitants of Murdering-Town*

"That's correct," Laerte said. "His father was brother to ours. We all grew up in Loreley."

"Curious how you all seem to have forenames with the last letter omitted," Athenor smiled. "Laerte instead of Laertes, Ulysse instead of Ulysses, and now Oreste instead of Orestes."

"A tradition in the Von Mardure family," Laerte grunted. "Said to be a token of good fortune."

"Your father's name?" pursued Athenor.

"Talo – short for Talos. His brother, Oreste's father, was named Atride instead of Atrides." When Athenor lifted a quizzical eyebrow, Laerte impatiently snapped, "An alternate name for Agamemnon. Didn't you study your Greek literature in school?"

"I hate to disappoint you, Judge, but I don't know everything." Athenor paused and then puckishly added, "Perhaps I should refer to you as 'Judg'?" (He pronounced it as "Judd -ugh").

Laerte shook his head irritably but fought down a smile regardless.

They fell into silence for a while, listening to the rain lash the French windows.

Finally, Ulysse muttered, "I never thought I'd return to Loreley. I thought I shook its dust from my heels long ago."

"That was your choice, no one else's." Laerte shook his finger at him. "No one cared too much when you decided to convert from the Lutheran Church to Catholicism."

"No one except our parents," Ulysse snapped. "It wasn't you that our mother cursed out. Anyway, if you liked Loreley so much, why didn't you stay?"

"Uh…I did not leave on happy terms with our tutor in the law, as you know full well. Considering that Judge Mietling essentially was *the* law in Pastorius County, I could have never gained the judgeship there that I wanted."

"Mietling was an arrogant cockwomble[6]," Ulysse muttered, "and worse. I'm sure no one mourns his death in 1753.".

At that, Athenor gazed somberly at Ulysse. Only the two of them knew the full story about Associate Judge Moritz Mietling – of how he murdered his wife and blamed his two servants for it, leading to their suicides.[7]

"Is Mietling's judgeship still vacant?" Archer asked.

Ulysse shook his head. "He was soon replaced, thank goodness. Not that I'd want to return permanently to Loreley, anyway. I'm going because Cousin Oreste has asked for help."

"The letter was informative," interjected Laerte, leaning back in his chair, eyes hooded. "It seems that the legendary ghosts of Loreley Town have emerged again. You remember, Ulysse?"

"Of course, brother. Just before we both left, they supposedly killed a trader on the road. Oh, they've been a staple of bedtime stories to frighten children for years…"

---

[6] Slang meaning an incredibly stupid and obnoxious man

[7] As related in *The Eighth Otter*

Ulysse trailed off into momentary silence. "Even before the founding of the town, local Lenape legends spoke of solitary travelers or tribespeople being killed, especially during the winter months, by something…or perhaps some*things*…"

"But this time, it's different," Laerte took up the thread. "Despite the departure of winter, the killings have continued – and not just in the open countryside, but in the town itself. The local authorities are reportedly their usual scoffing selves, ridiculing any who give credence to the legend. Privately, they're not so blind as to deny the existence of such things as ghosts, but insist they need no help in dealing with whatever might be happening."

"But your reputation precedes you, Doctor." Laerte gestured at Athenor. "The Pastorius County Shrievalty[8] may be too proud to ask your help, but Oreste has his finger on the pulse of his congregants and most of the ordinary townsfolk."

"They are thankful you accepted their plea," Ulysse said. "And I'm personally grateful to have you with me on the journey. Obviously, Laerte can't go, but *I* must – we still have family there."

"Did Oreste mention anything else?" Archer asked. "Like what these ghosts are supposed to be? Ghosts of humans? Or something else? And did he say anything about how the victims were killed?"

Laerte leaned forward to steeple his fingers on the desk. He gazed at the leaping flames in the hearth for a moment before answering. "There are legends. But no one has yet

---

[8] What the office of a sheriff is called

survived to tell what manner of creatures they are. And the bodies of the victims are…all ashen and bluish as if somehow drained. Not of blood or fluid or flesh, but seemingly of the breath of life itself."

Raindrops trickled down the chimney to quietly hiss and sputter in the fire.

2. The Meeting

White tatters of cloud drifted in the chilly blue sky above
the mountains that bracketed Loreley Town. The town lay
in a broad valley, which the Lenape called *Scahentiarrhonon* –
too difficult a word for the German and Dutch townsfolk,
who preferred their name of Loreley Valley. The mountain
ranges that marched in a north-to-south direction similarly
had Lenape names – the *Linchen Kihatënink* and *Achpateuny
Kihatënink* – which meant "East Wind" and "West Wind"
Mountains, respectively. Predictably, the townspeople
preferred the translations. There was also a tree-flanked river
that ran from northeast to southwest through the center
of the green, hilly town, again with its own Lenape name
– *Lechauwa-hannek* – which had long ago been discarded in
favor of *Paradiesfluss* or Paradise River.

In truth, the German and Dutch settlers who founded
the town in 1700 believed they had arrived in a heavenly land.
There was abundant land for farming, forested mountains for
hunting and trapping, and brown trout and bass in the cool
river. The local Lenape were friendly and became reliable
trading partners in short order. Eventually, the settlement
became a town of more than 700 families – tradesmen, farmers
and their workers, artisans, laborers, and even several lawyers
who transacted affairs for county residents at the town
Courthouse. From its modest beginnings, the courthouse
had developed an enviable reputation and enough legal
business to warrant both a Chief Judge, Maximilian Lindt,
and a new Associate Judge, Simon Groat (who had replaced
Moritz Mietling).

Although there were scattered farms, hamlets, and cabins in the general area, Loreley Town became the seat of what came to be called Pastorius County. It was named in honor of the early German émigré Franz Pastorius, who founded a settlement just north of Philadelphia that was prosaically named Germantown. Even before he died, in 1700 some of his disciples left to establish their own settlement in the northeast of His Majesty's Province of Pennsylvania. Like Pastorius, they were mostly Lutheran [9], but with some adherents of the Reformed Church.

Notable among them was former Royal Prussian Navy officer Heinrich Kühleborn. The watchtower he built on the high north hill of town, the *Seemansturm* or Seaman's Tower, still pierced the high clouds and cast its shadow on the green-painted rooftops. At its foot was the sumptuous house of the wealthy town physician, Athaulf Kitzler, who also had a clinic near the center of town.

The town's name derived, of course, from the German legend of the Lorelei – the enchantress who lured mariners to their doom. In christening it, the town founders were thinking only of the "enchantment" part of the myth.

But it was not long before the "doom" part began to make itself known. Not suddenly, but only occasionally and gradually and only during the winter months – something that could be ignored or rationalized.

Up to now.

---

[9] However, Pastorius was rumored to have quietly converted to Quakerism before his death in 1720.

Some of this history passed through Pastor Oreste von Mardure's thoughts as he hurried through the park in the center of town toward the German Reformed Church. This was not his church, of course — that was the Saint Boniface Lutheran Church in the southwest, where the river finally exited the town and continued to eventually join the larger Susquehanough River.

If anyone noticed him, they would have seen a clean-shaven man of about sixty years, with only streaks of gray in his thinning brown hair, long bushy sideburns, a little under average height, with a craggy face. He was dressed — as all gentlemen in town were — in the usual brown coat with tails, knee-breeches, calf-stockings, and polished buckle-shoes. His tan waistcoat concealed both a white cotton shirt and a slightly protuberant belly.

There had been rain last night, and some of it still glistened on the yellowish leaves of the silver maple trees shading the winding dirt path. As he emerged from the park, he saw some townsfolk about — housewives on their way to the Market House in the northeast or tradesmen strolling into the Tatzelwürm Rathskeller for their mid-day dinner. There were even a few Lenape men dressed in Native garb, whom no one gave a second glance.

Following the riverbank with its many wooden bridges, he passed by several fishers, both men and boys, with their wooden poles in the slowly moving waters. The Paradise River was still known for its abundance of trout, bass, and walleye.

An excited cry drew his attention and he saw two barefoot teen youths dancing on the bank, struggling to pull in their catch.

He paused to watch as the line gradually rose from the water and a fiercely squirming four-foot-long creature broke the surface. It had a long, narrow snout and when its jaws gaped, rows of sharp teeth were snapping. The boys groaned with dismay and while one struggled with the pole, the other produced a knife and cut the line. The creature fell back into the water with a tremendous splash and then squirmed under and vanished.

"Are you *jungen* all right?" Oreste called.

They were cursing but when they recognized the Lutheran pastor, they stopped and smiled sheepishly. "Yes, yes, Pastor. Just lost some good fishing line is all," one replied.

"Alligator gar?" Oreste knew that those reptiles were rare in these parts but still quite dangerous – and even though they could grow to a length of ten feet, were not worth the effort to catch.

"No wonder the fishing's been poor lately," the other boy grumbled. "That devil's been eating them all."

By that time, adult fishermen had come up and joined the conversation, and Oreste heard talk about hunting the gar down and spearing it. Assured that the boys were all right, Oreste silently drew away and continued along the riverbank.

At length, he arrived at the center of town, the Town Square where the Hop-Toad Road had its terminus. He gazed dolefully at the ruined building adjacent to the river's edge.

The recent fire had gutted the Town Hall, leaving only tilted sooty chimneys rising amid jagged fragments of walls. The stairways had pulled loose from their bolts and nails and led up to an open sky cross-crossed with broken and blackened roof beams. At the bottom was a squat ashy heap where the rubble of offices and their furnishings lay. The whole place stank of wet charcoal. The only sounds were the skitters of the rats and the lizards in the ruins.

The stone foundation still seemed sound but why not? That foundation was the oldest structure in town – already existent when the first settlers arrived. Even to this day, no one had a guess who built it or when. It was upon that foundation that the Town Hall was erected. Now it was barely all that was left.

It was thought that the chimneys had developed leaks, permitting hot embers to fester in the wooden walls and ignite them. No one was hurt, but most of the town records – deeds, land grants, appointments to office, and Town Council records – were destroyed. Fortunately, legal records such as liens, wills, lawsuits, and criminal prosecutions were stored in the Pastorius County Courthouse, and there thus spared.

Ordinarily, a meeting like today's would have been held at the Town Hall, but now the German church had to substitute. Here, the leading townsmen, including the Town Council, mayor, and sheriff had gathered to discuss the recent killings.

The last echoes of the summoning church bells died away, and ahead of him, Oreste saw a few townsmen entering the white-painted wooden building, with its gabled roofs and steeple and its 30-foot-high bell tower.

He saw the frail figure of the German church pastor, Baldur Rathenau, wobbling on his cane at the entrance, nodding and shaking hands with the men filing inside. Despite being pastors of rival churches and their theological differences, the two were close friends, and he felt a twinge of concern at Rathenau's sickly appearance. He was about fifty years old, but thin and frail, and had recently begun to lose his prematurely white hair.

Baldur's wife Bella was standing alongside him with a steadying arm under his elbow. She would not be coming inside – the meeting was for the townsmen alone, but Oreste was glad to see her lending Baldur a hand.

As Oreste approached the entrance, he glimpsed Dr. Kitzler, come from around the corner. As usual, he was dressed fastidiously, tricorn in hand, with a sturdy, erect carriage. His bright blond hair was brushed back from a commanding face with a pointed mustache. He looked more like a soldier than a physician. Upon reaching Baldur, he made a slight bow, gesturing with his hat, and smiling superciliously.

Baldur blinked uncomfortably, and as Oreste drew near, he realized that the doctor was exchanging his glance with Bella, not her husband. She frowned and broke eye contact with him. Kitzler inclined his head, replaced his hat, and sauntered inside.

"…does he have against me?" Baldur was whispering fiercely to Bella as Oreste came up.

"Hush," she replied sternly. "It's your imagination, that's all."

They turned to greet Oreste. A smile lit Baldur's wan face and he extended his hand for a warm handclasp. Bella just eyed him coolly and muttered her hello. She was a shapely woman with dark hair confined by a white bonnet, whose attractive face held a customarily solemn expression.

Oreste had long known that Bella did not care for him – or for his wife, Johanna, who returned the sentiment. But at least, he thought, Bella seemed to take pains to tend to her ailing husband. After all, she could have stayed at home instead of helping him hobble from their nearby parsonage.

"I think that's everyone who's coming." Oreste turned his head to scan the area. "Maybe it's time you were seated inside, Baldur."

Baldur gave a short nod and pecked Bella on the cheek. She gingerly released his elbow.

"I'll stop by the Market House, dear." Her voice was toneless. "I'm making that sauerkraut soup you like for our supper."

"My thanks." Baldur patted her cheek, and she turned to bow her head politely to Oreste and then hurried around the corner of the church, gathering her shawl about her shoulders.

Oreste hesitated to offer his friend a hand, knowing his pride about accepting another man's help (his wife's help was a different matter). But he kept close as the painfully thin pastor carefully maneuvered through the door, which a stoic congregant then closed behind them.

Together, they made their way down the aisle between the pews to the front, where a railing separated the chancel from the nave. Beyond was the linen-draped altar and a tall, plain cross fixed to the far wall between two tall windows. At one side, a staircase led to the elevated pulpit. The noontime light cascading through the nave's many windows made lighting the candle-chandeliers unnecessary.

As they passed by Dr. Kitzler's pew, Oreste glanced down in time to see the physician raise a condescending eyebrow at him. Oreste refrained from saying anything but wondered if Baldur might be right – Kitzler did not like him.

That Kitzler was Baldur's physician made that especially concerning. Over the past year or so, Baldur had become progressively weaker, barely able to stand by himself, even with his cane. He complained of joint pain and was chronically constipated. More worrisome, he had started to have convulsions – not frequently, but the mere fact of them was cause for worry.

But Kitzler reportedly had not the slightest idea what ailment was responsible. Even more troubling, the good doctor did not seem very concerned about it. True, he usually preferred hobnobbing with the wealthy elite to the care of his patients, but his specific indifference to Baldur's health was puzzling.

Dismissing thoughts of that for the moment, Oreste seated himself in the front pew beside Baldur, whose breath came raggedly after his exertion. Glancing past Baldur along the pew, he saw the corpulent town mayor, Gerben Schreur, replete with a white scratch-wig that did not hide the few scraggles of hair at his nape. It was well-known the mayor was mostly bald, having only a meager fringe around the sides and back of his head. It was equally well-known that he was quite vain – and not merely about his looks but his competencies as well. However, more than one wag had suggested he was vain "without much to be vain about."

Seated next to the mayor was Chief Judge Maximilian Lindt, immaculately dressed, his thinning white hair meticulously brushed back from a high forehead. From his cadaverous appearance, one would never guess that he suffered from gout – until they saw how painfully he hobbled on his cane. Like most of the well-to-do citizens, he was a personal patient of Kitzler, rather than his nurses.

The judge exchanged a brief look with Oreste and the dark eyes beneath his overhanging brow did not blink. That was not unusual for the judge, and sometimes Oreste imagined those eyes to be ever sizing people up for a noose. Beside him sat his bailiff, the portly Timon Bierhals – a name that meant "beer-drinker." He lived up to it but seemed reasonably sober today.

On the other side of Bierhals was a pale, scrawny man of middle-age, with thinning hair that seemed more like a sprinkle of grayish dust. His habitually dour expression did not change, and he made no acknowledgment of Oreste. This was Associate Judge Simon Groat, a modest but dedicated jurist without much ambition.

Beyond him, Pastorius County Sheriff Egon Richter got to his feet. He was a sturdy middle-aged man with a florid face, bulbous nose, and a truncated goatee. Oreste had to stifle a smile when gazing at the sheriff's ears, which almost seemed to sprout beards of their own along the rims. He was dressed in a bottle-green coat. The tricorn he held in hand was of the same color and emblazoned with the town crest – a river winding between two mountain ranges.

Mayor Schreur exchanged a glance with Richter and together they rose to their feet and proceeded to the railing. For a moment of alarm, Oreste thought they were going to set foot into the sacred ground of the cancel, but they stopped short to turn and face the audience.

The crowd was still a sea of voices talking to and over each other. Schreur gestured to Bierhals, who ponderously rose, clasping his three-foot-long courtroom tipstaff. He banged it on the floor, eliciting a wince from Baldur, but managing to quiet the audience.

As their babble subsided, Schreur lifted his arms to address them.

"Gentlemen, my thanks for coming today. I know most of you are eager to be about your business, so this meeting will be brief." He paused to survey the faces before him – some intense, others worried, more that were bland and indifferent, and a few that were impatient. "We're here because some of you have raised an alarm about the recent deaths and have demanded better protection from our shrievalty. Rather than address your concerns individually, I've asked Sheriff Richter to speak to you all…" He gestured at the man next to him and then stepped back a pace.

Richter cleared his throat and forced what he hoped would be a reassuring smile. "You all know the history of the winter deaths– they've been happening for as long as memory serves. The legend of the *Wintergeister* – the 'Winter Ghosts' predates the town's founding.

"Solitary travelers in the countryside have sometimes been found dead, their corpses blue and grayish. You all know the legend – believed by the credulous – that some malevolent unearthly creatures are responsible. I'm here to tell you that it's nonsense…" When some of the townsmen began to mutter in objection, Richter waved a mollifying hand. "None of the bodies have ever had any marks of violence on them. Yes, they died of some malady, but there has never been any physical evidence of murder. Doctor…?" He gestured at Kitzler, who rose serenely and faced the audience.

"I'm a well-trained physician, as you all know," he began smoothly. "I've seen bodies killed by murder and many more that have been killed by illness or disease. Sheriff Richter asked me to examine those recent bodies people have been chattering about – *Herr und Frau* Huber, who were found with their sleigh on the way into town one February morning. Anna Huber had been under my care during her pregnancy, and it appears that they had been hurrying into town. My autopsy showed that Anna was miscarrying. But between her blood loss, the emotional strain on Rudolf Huber's heart, and the freezing weather, their deaths are completely explicable…"

"And what about *Jungfer*[10] Gertrude Vogt? She was a member of my congregation." Baldur interrupted. "She was found in the same condition as those bodies, but in her garret – not outside. And pardon me for saying so, but at the age of 59 was unlikely to be miscarrying."

———————————

[10] spinster

A ripple of laughter swept through the audience before Richter batted his hands downward for silence. Kitzler gave Baldur a look of barely concealed anger, and his voice took on an edge.

"The charwoman? Did you know she was a patient of mine? It might also interest you that she was in poor health for several years. Especially cleaning virtually all the offices in the Town Hall alone – backbreaking work. She was almost relieved when it burned down. So, she scarcely had a hearty disposition."

He smiled smugly at Baldur. "But, yes, Pastor, she was not outside. However, the fire in her stove had gone out and when she was found, it was quite cold in that attic. So, again, I say it was a natural death. Might I remind all of you," he raised his eyes to scan the audience, "that none of these bodies had marks of violence, there was no blood that was shed, no flesh that was pierced, cut, or shot. None! Now, unless any of you are a physician, I would ask that you trust someone who is."

"But surely," Oreste interjected, turning slightly to view the audience, "any physician would welcome a second opinion from another physician to verify their conclusions."

As Kitlzer struggled to contain his exasperation, Schreur stepped forward and lifted a hand. "Yes, of course, Pastor von Mardure. I'm sure Dr. Kitzler would be open to that – especially since you've already sent for one, I understand."

Oreste stood up and faced the audience. "A while ago, I sent a missive to my cousins in Leichtenberg. You know them – the brothers Laerte and Ulysse von Mardure. I had heard that the town physician from Dereham had joined them there. Some of you might have heard of him – Seth Athenor…"

A murmur ran through the audience, some of it affirmative, some disparaging.

"You mean that jumped-up chemist?" Kitzler snapped. "He's not even a medical college graduate!"

"But he has faced and defeated several menaces before," expostulated Oreste. "Some of you might know people who still remember the Droitwijk Terror of 1752, for instance."

"We all heard of that – at least wild stories of it," Richter harumphed. "But even if some of it truly happened, my understanding is that it was defeated by an Abenaki shaman – not Athenor."

"Dr. Athenor never claimed credit and always championed the shaman's critical role," Oreste responded. "But those in the know told me that the doctor did substantially contribute to the Terror's defeat – and helped defeat other supernatural menaces elsewhere.

"Surely, we can all agree in this enlightened age that true demons and monsters exist! Admittedly, in the past, some innocent souls have been wrongly accused of witchery and the like, but that does not disprove the existence of genuine witches and demons."

"Those wretches hanged in Massachusetts Bay *were* witches, I say!" Richter snorted. "I know it's very fashionable to proclaim their innocence some sixty years later."

"Then, you *do* agree that supernatural menaces exist," Oreste retorted. "Such as the Winter Ghosts." While Richter fought down his visible irritation, he continued, "The point I'm making is that there'll be no harm in asking Dr. Athenor here to lend us the wisdom of his experience…if that's all right by you?"

Richter's face flushed and he was about to say something when Judge Lindt carefully rose, leaning on his cane, which he banged on the floor for attention.

"I wish to add my voice in favor of Dr. Athenor's help. If no one else has, I've heard of his endeavors in Dereham Town last year to rid it of a supernatural menace and…" he paused, "to solve an old murder that happened here in Loreley.[11] I can say no more about that. But I, for one, hold Dr. Athenor's reputation in high regard."

An approving murmur ran through the crowd and Mayor Schreur, sensing the sentiment, touched Richter's elbow to silence him.

"Of course, there is no harm in having Dr. Athenor come." He said oleaginously. "Especially since he is already on his way, I understand."

Kitzler darted him a disapproving glance, then pursed his lips and strode irritably back to his pew.

"In the meantime," Schreur fiddled with his scratch-wig, "let us all keep calm. Surely…now that winter is over, we have little to worry about at present. Those deaths have never happened during the other seasons."

------

[11] As related in *The Eighth Otter*

Oreste was about to bring up the fact that Gertrude Vogt had died only last month, after the last of the snows, but realized it would be useless.

The audience gave their general assent, and Schreur gestured for them to disperse. They filed out down the aisle toward the front door, and as he passed by, Schreur gave Oreste a patronizing pat on the shoulder. Oreste forced a polite smile but made no such effort when Kitzler marched by to glower at him. Richter did not bother looking at him at all.

Finally, all that remained were the two pastors and some of the church factotums who went about cleaning up after the audience. The pastors sat in silence for a time, then Oreste turned to Baldur.

"Did you get a chance to discover much at the Town Hall before it burned?"

"Not much, I'm afraid." Baldur smiled weakly. "As you know, I was hoping to learn more about the Winter Ghosts from old records, but of late I've been too weak to do very much."

"That leaves us with few other avenues to pursue." Oreste rubbed his jaw meditatively. "There are several oldsters who might remember something. For instance, did you ever have a chance to speak with Gertrude before her death?"

"No," Baldur answered quickly, dropping his eyes.

Oreste did not notice that and continued, "You know, I have a mind to travel to Cloud Village to see what can be learned from the Lenape."

"But they don't like you very much, or at least my fellow pastor there doesn't."

"Nikolasz Schraal? Yes, I know he dislikes me. The feeling is mutual."

"And I'm no longer in his favor either, despite our shared faith." Baldur sighed. "He was not always so taciturn. After the death of his wife ten years ago, he became embittered."

"Do you have any influence or oversight on his congregation? Something that will bend him to my visiting them there?"

Baldur shook his head. "Although we belong to the same church, we are two separate congregations. Nominally, the Reformed Assembly in Philadelphia has oversight on both of us, but even they cannot force a pastor's hospitality."

"Hmm." That did not come as a surprise to Oreste. "I've seen him here about town sometimes, prowling around like a ghoul. Does he ever call on you?"

"Hardly ever now. We used to meet quite often, but then for the past year or two, his visits grew fewer and fewer. He would occasionally stop by to borrow a hymnal or to share a glass of my wine." Baldur smiled thinly. "Probably more for the latter than the former. But even that tapered off and stopped altogether, although he has continued to come to town, as you said."

"Come to think of it," Oreste paused in remembrance, "I saw him in town only a little while back, headed into the tobacconist shop. You can always tell when he's about, by the stink of his pipe. Or maybe it's his own stench." His craggy face broke into a mischievous grin.

"You did not greet him, I suppose."

"No. No sense in that, considering how he feels about me."

"Then you can hardly expect much welcome or cooperation at Cloud Village." Baldur sighed. "Whatever they know, they've long since shared with Schraal – there is no one who knows more about the ghosts than he."

"But there might still be some Lenape oldsters who remember things of importance," Oreste persisted. "I'd still like to question any who would cooperate with me."

Baldur shrugged. "If I were stronger, I would go with you to try. But perhaps you should wait until Dr. Athenor arrives. He might get a better reception there than you. Surely, Schraal has not poisoned the minds of the tribespeople about *him*."

"Maybe you're right." Oreste's irritation subsided. "But in addition to giving another opinion about the deaths, I'd like Athenor to give a second opinion about your health as well."

Baldur patted his friend's hand gratefully and gave a crooked smile. "Let's hope I'm still alive when he arrives."

They fell silent again, meditatively gazing at the light streaming in broad yellow swathes from the high windows. Finally, Oreste frowned and met his friend's eyes.

"Do you believe what Kitzler said? About those people dying from the cold?"

"No. You might be able to argue that for the victims found in the snowfields. But what about poor Gertrude Vogt? Not in the winter countryside under an open sky like the others." Baldur raised his eyes to the solemn cross fixed to the wall of his church. "But in the spring and…here in town and under her own roof."

3. The Village in the Clouds

The dirt trail climbed through the forested hills, zigzagging through the trees, and skirting rock ledges and outcroppings. After ascending about 300 feet, the two men stopped to dismount and rest their horses. Seth Athenor held firmly to the reins of his skittish mare and spoke some soothing words to her. At his side, Ulysse von Mardure knuckled his back and cursed softly, glaring at his gelding.

Athenor eyed him with faint amusement. "It seems you like horses less than I do."

"They're the stupidest creatures God ever made," rasped the former lawyer. "Except for the six cabbages seated in a jury box."

"It's only a little further to the village." Athenor pointed up the trail, where it wound amid the green pine and blue spruce. They could see the sharp top of a palisade partly shrouded by a white haze. "It looks like we're almost there."

"I'm just glad we traveled this far without running into bandits or renegades."

"If we had, I'm sure your penknife would have given them a fright," Athenor had not forgotten how Ulysse had carried that around during the fights with the vampires in Leichtenberg but had never used it despite his expectation. That had become a running joke with Laerte, who never tired of teasing his brother about it.

Ulysse's face flushed but he made no reply. Athenor tried to hide a smile.

He looked back down the trail, where it vanished into the April forest. From their elevation, they could see the plain dotted with thickets of hemlock, oak, and pine and the dusty thread that was the Hop-Toad Road. Paralleling it was the tree-lined Paradise River and in the distance was the darkening ridge of the West Wind Mountains. Shadowy clouds had gathered above them and were slowly edging east. Only a few orange glimmers of the sunset broke through their mauve folds like dying embers.

"Looks like a storm is brewing up," Athenor observed. "We could never have made Loreley Town tonight. Your memory of the way from Leichtenberg proved true."

"Hmph," was Ulysse's only response as he stiffly remounted.

The physician followed his example, and they trotted up the trail. Through the fogs, they could also make out where the forested hills changed into mountains – the East Wind Mountains that marched along this side of the valley. They were not high – only about 2000 feet – but Athenor was glad that the Lenape village was not further up.

He searched his memory for what he knew about the Lenape. Their name meant "The People." He knew they detested the name that most Provincials gave them, "The Delaware." That name was coined in honor of an English lord to designate the river in southeastern Pennsylvania

Province[12] Yet, that was where many Lenape originally lived before succumbing to pressure to emigrate further west in the aftermath of disease, famine, and war.

They spoke an Algonquian variant and were known to prefer being peaceable but could field fierce warriors when necessary. Some tribes had accepted Christianity, most recently those living in southeastern Pennsylvania, near the Moravian-founded town of Bethlehem. Under the guidance of missionaries, they had turned from wigwams and longhouses to European-style houses and buildings, and some had even adopted Provincial-style clothing. In that sense, they were like the Mohawks Athenor had met near Leichtenberg, although those professed an Anglican faith.

From what Ulysse had told him on the trip, *Kùmhòkunk* had been evangelized by German Reformed missionaries shortly after Loreley was founded. But, astonishingly enough, the village already had European-style houses and buildings – but who had designed them or when they were built, no one could say.

Athenor and Ulysse proceeded through the forest, and above the twitter of birds and the chatter of scolding squirrels, they could hear the splash of rushing water. Athenor realized that the village must be near some source of fresh water, such as a mountain brook or stream.

Finally, the trail ended in a large meadow where the wooden palisade marched across the yellow and blue

---

[12] In 1682, Pennsylvania was granted the territory on the western coast of Delaware Bay, and until 1776 this was called the "Lower Counties on the Delaware." Although semi-autonomous, it still answered to the Royal Governor of Pennsylvania Province.

flowered ground. Above the open gates was a parapet where two sentries stood with their muskets. Some fishermen were filtering inside for the night, with poles draped over their shoulders, and sacks bulging with their daily catches. There were also women returning from that hidden stream or brook with their laundry in wicker baskets.

None wore Provincial-style clothing, presumably disdained as impractical in the wilderness. The men wore garments of fringed deerskin – leggings and overshirt – as well as moccasins. Unlike those tribes that remained devoted to their Native beliefs, they had not shaved their heads, but wore their hair long, tied with a leather ribbon at the back. The women similarly wore calf-length deerskin wraparound skirts and beaded blouses, some with wampum necklaces. They did not have braided hair but wore it long and flowing.

A few darted glances of curiosity, but they did not seem alarmed by the presence of strangers.

The two travelers swung down from their horses and led them by the reins up to the gate. One of the sentries leaned over the parapet to inspect them.

"Are you from town?" His tone held no suspiciousness, only polite interest.

"No," Athenor replied, meeting his eyes. "But that's where we're bound. We've come from New York Province. My friend…" he gestured at Ulysse, "is cousin to the Lutheran pastor in Loreley."

The sentry's face momentarily clouded but he waved them inside without further words.

Ulysse did not miss the sentry's reaction and edged alongside Athenor as they proceeded inside.

"I don't think letting the villagers know we have Lutheran affiliation is a good idea," he whispered. "I was raised in Loreley Town, remember? This village is loyal to the German Reformed Church, and they are resistant to any perceived attempts at assimilation by the Lutherans…Not as much from theological differences as territoriality."

"In that case," Athenor returned wryly, "we had best not let on that we are both Catholics."

Ulysse scowled with exasperation at that obvious suggestion.

As they trotted along, they gazed about with interest at the European-style housing. It was not as elaborate as the structures in Loreley Town but still consisted of squarish wooden houses of horizontal logs, with peaked roofs and stone chimneys. Some of them had two stories, and all had diamond-pane glass windows with plain shutters. Most structures were of unpainted wood. The exception was the church in the center of the village, which was white with three tall windows on each of its rectangular sides and one in the steeple between the two front doors. The steeple rose to a point-topped bell tower.

As they plodded near, Athenor noticed that the white color came from whitewash. He could not help remembering Saint Paul's remark in *Acts* about hypocrites being akin to "whitewashed walls."

Even as that thought entered his mind, he saw two people emerge from one of the front doors. One was a young male with a friendly demeanor, the other an older man whose stern face was marked by the lines of what must have been longstanding captiousness. He was dressed all in somber brown, and his hatless head had a few meager black strands brushed back from his tall forehead. He had a short chin-curtain beard stretching from ear to ear, black sprinkled with white. His upper lip was shaven.

He noticed the newcomers and inspected them suspiciously as they dismounted.

"And who might you be, strangers?" he challenged in a rumble of a voice. He spoke in English, which was not unexpected, since that tongue was increasingly the *lingua-franca* of all British North America, eclipsing regional Dutch or German and even the Native languages.

Ulysse seemed about to respond with equal asperity, but Athenor touched his elbow and forced a smile.

"We are from Leichtenberg in New York Province," he said placidly. "We are bound for Loreley Town but did not want to continue in the dark…We were wondering if you would be so kind as to offer shelter for the night."

The man seemed about to refuse when the younger man returned Athenor's smile. "Of course. We would not refuse shelter to fellow Christians. Wouldn't we, Pastor Schraal?"

The older man pursed his lips irritably, then gave a shrug of acquiescence. "Of course, of course. It is not good to travel at night in these parts. My deacon here is quite right. We would be remiss in our Biblical duty to refuse you."

"Without meaning to pry," the deacon added, "Might I ask what faith you two practice?"

"We are both Anglican — as are some in Leichtenberg," Ulysse lied. He thought that naming a faith neither Lutheran nor Catholic might be the safest course for the moment.

"Hmm," Schraal responded non-committedly, "at least you're Protestant."

Athenor hid a smile, silently congratulating Ulysse on his shrewdness.

The deacon stepped forward and extended a hand to Athenor. "My name is Gabriël Martens, and this..." he waved his other hand back at the church, "is the East Wind Reformed Church."

Athenor took his hand and found it to be firm but warm and introduced him and Ulysse. At the mention of Ulysse's last name, Gabriël arched an eyebrow.

"You have some family in Loreley, then," He made it a statement rather than a question.

"Yes, it is the Von Mardure family seat, although there are relatives in New York Province as well," Ulysse replied without defensiveness.

As Martens went to shake with Ulysse, Athenor could hardly miss that Schraal made no similar gesture. The pastor merely stood with arms akimbo and a sour expression. When Martens went on to invite the two to lodge at his own house, Athenor could scarcely keep from sighing aloud with relief.

"Well," the pastor said grudgingly, "welcome to *Kùmhòkunk*." Pivoting on his heel, he retreated inside the church and shut the door firmly behind him.

Gabriël looked a bit embarrassed but made no comment. He led the way to the right of the church where the open doors of the village stables waited. They saw the blacksmith at the adjacent smithy closing his shop for the night, a typical burly man with massive arms — also a Lenape. There was a wiry oldster, with long, grayish hair who proclaimed himself the stablemaster.

He helped the two place their horses into the straw-filled stalls, where water troughs were already filled, and hay was piled beside them. Alongside the wall were a series of other stalls, with several horses being tended by an adolescent boy.

Athenor was about to remove his mare's saddle and harness, but the stablemaster lightly swatted his hand away.

"I'll have young Joshua see to that, sir," he said, "and make sure they're all washed and brushed." He gestured to a cask of water and various brushes, towels, and hoof picks.

Athenor smiled at the stablemaster's solicitude, and when the latter refused his offer of coin, inclined his head with gratitude. Gabriël led them outside and in the direction of the church. As they passed along its side, they noticed a small attached single-story cabin, where lamplight suddenly bloomed in its windows.

"That is Pastor Schraal's parsonage," Gabriël explained. "He's likely missing supper tonight to study."

"Not a very lavish parsonage," Ulysse whispered to Athenor, trying to hide the scorn in his voice.

"I seem to recall you didn't exactly live in a mansion yourself back in Dereham," Athenor whispered back sardonically. He was being deliberate in his use of "mansion," since that was what Ulysse's mayor's house was called, even though it was scarcely any larger or more lavish than Schraal's.

"Our pastor is a very dedicated man," Gabriël explained, oblivious to the exchange. "He studies long into the night – not merely to prepare sermons, but to improve his knowledge. He has assembled quite a collection of old books and manuscripts."

"Does he have a family?" Athenor asked.

Gabriël's face clouded momentarily. "He used to have a wife, Rosamund. She died about ten years ago."

"My condolences," Athenor murmured, genuinely sympathetic. He knew what it was like to lose a beloved wife.

Gabriël inclined his head a fraction, and Athenor sensed there was more that the deacon wanted to disclose but could not. He let the matter drop but filed away that bit of information.

"My friend Ulysse is a scholar as well," Athenor offered as a change of subject.

Ulysse seemed to be doleful, wrapped in his thoughts. Athenor eyed him contemplatively. Did the mention of a lost love resonate with the former lawyer, too? Ulysse had been notoriously closed-mouthed about his personal history, and Athenor had never sought to pry. Ulysse had always professed to be a lifelong bachelor – but it was certainly possible that there was more to it than that…

Athenor dismissed such thoughts. It was none of his business. Ulysse was a friend, not a patient.

The former lawyer blinked and roused himself from his reverie. "It comes with the legal profession," he muttered with embarrassment.

They all then fell silent as they continued east through the village, noticing that it was laid out on the slope of the hill, tiers of houses rising higher and higher toward the sheltering mountains. The village was longer than it was wide, surrounded by tall stockades on all sides.

Athenor supposed it could not be otherwise. Even with the proximate German town and the nominal protection of the Iroquois, it had to rely on its own defenses, especially with the prospect of war from nearby French-allied Cayuga and Oneida tribes.

They passed by thickets of oak and some apple trees here and there. Gabriël pointed out several vegetable gardens, the storage house, and the smokehouse. There was even a small sweat lodge, but that was mainly used by the elderly men of the village. Gabriël also explained that near the local brook – the *Wachtschu Siputët* or Mountain Stream – were the corn, bean, and squash fields. Those "three sisters" were ubiquitous throughout Native settlements in British America and Canada.

Finally, they arrived at a modest two-story cottage, where white smoke wisped from the chimney at the side of its peaked roof. They noticed someone at the foot of an apple tree nearby.

Athenor paused to have a closer look, and at his elbow, Ulysse gave a start of surprise. For, a man dressed in a tattered cotton shirt and knee-breeches without socks or shoes was dancing around the trunk. His unconfined long black hair whirled and tossed as he capered, oblivious to their presence.

"Hans!" Gabriël called indulgently. "No apple buds until next month. Come inside. I want you to meet someone."

"No, no, no," The man chattered with a silly grin. Athenor saw that despite his antics, his right leg and arm seemed weak in comparison with the left.

"Why not, brother? Supper is ready." Gabriël was bewildered.

"Supper, supper, supper…" Hans echoed ecstatically. But he did not move, and Athenor wondered if he understood or was just mindlessly echoing the word.

The deacon lifted a hand in surrender and guided Athenor and Ulysse to the door and opened it to usher them inside. They found themselves in a sitting room paneled with polished cedar and a floor of firm oak planks. To the left was a modest fire in the hearth, and nearby was a set of steps leading to the second floor. In the center of the room was a circular table, surrounded by chairs. In one corner was a larder with a hinged door on top. There was a door nearby leading to the pantry.

"Your brother?" Ulysse gave a curious glance back outside as Gabriël shut the door.

"Yes. My older brother. He was born like that — right side all weak and not a wit in his head," he replied without embarrassment. "Cannot speak much for the most part… Maybe a word he repeats over and over, usually something he's just heard. But there are times…"

"Harmless?" Ulysse raised a doubtful eyebrow.

"Oh, yes. He's never been a danger to any. On the contrary, we adults must be stern with some children who mock him…They call him *Verrückt* Hans — 'Daft Hans.' But he was given a good soul — if not a matching body."

"I'm glad to hear you're watching out for him," Athenor remarked. "Is it just the two of you?"

"No, we live with an elderly Lenape woman, named Cholena." Gabriël gestured at the stairs in one corner. "She is the oldest living villager…"

"As opposed to the oldest dead villager, I guess," Ulysse grumbled to himself. Athenor nudged him in the ribs.

If he noticed that remark, the deacon made no sign. "She might be 100 years old but has no children or other relatives. So, I took her under my roof some years ago to care for her. She is quite wise — highly intelligent, in fact — and spiritual, although she has never accepted baptism. She prays to *Ketanëtuwit* — the Lenape Creator, who may or not be equivalent to God the Father."

"Interesting," Athenor said. "She must know quite a lot about local history. I'd enjoy speaking with her about it."

The deacon's face turned somber. "I'm afraid she has been unable to speak for the last few years. Dr. Kitzler examined her and said she had something called apoplexia."[13]

"Unfortunate," Athenor replied with genuine sympathy. "How does she communicate? Does she know how to write?"

"I taught her English before her ailment. She used to speak it fluently. But…" he paused uncertainly, "I know you will think this mad. Now, Hans has always spent a lot of time with her. Our mother died many years ago, and I suppose in his mind Chelona is something of a substitute…"

"And I suppose I'm a bit famished, *Herr* Martens," Ulysse gazed down at the bare dining table.

Athenor winced at his friend's obtuseness, but Gabriël continued imperturbably,

"…They are quite fond of each other. Sometimes… sometimes he will say something that gives me a start. Like the name of a person who died before he was born and sometimes can speak in fluent sentences when he is with her. At those times, his eyes become vacant, and his echoic speech leaves him, and he can relate an event from long ago. An event which he certainly never witnessed or even one that most villagers remember."

"What do you make of that?" Athenor already had an idea forming.

"That Cholena is able to use Hans as a kind of conduit for her thoughts. That they are spiritually linked in some

---

[13] What a cerebrovascular accident – stroke – was called in those days.

unguessable way." The deacon shrugged away his perplexity. "I know Pastor Schraal believes so. He has spent long hours sitting with them both, asking questions and listening to Hans give answers – intelligent answers, using an educated vocabulary. But the words that come from his slack mouth are not his."

"Indeed?" Athenor tried to ignore Ulysse's antics – he almost seemed to be hopping from one foot to the other. *Ravenous or just needing to relieve himself?* He wondered dryly. "Pastor Schraal must be an exceedingly kind and patient man to favor them with such undivided attention."

Gabriël blinked nervously, clearly struggling not to say anything uncomplimentary about his superior. "He is very interested in local legends and history…" He broke off to motion them to seats at the table and then disappeared into the pantry. A moment later, he reappeared with three mugs in the crook of an elbow and a glass demijohn in the other hand. He managed to set the mugs down on the table with the help of Athenor and began to fill them from the demijohn.

"Corn whiskey," he announced as he poured. "We make it ourselves – although we buy these bottles from Loreley merchants who visit us." He then fetched a clay jug of water, and they all added it to their whiskey. It took a strong stomach to drink neat something that was about 80% alcohol. Gabriël went back to the larder and produced a platter with a loaf of cornbread flavored with maple sugar. He proceeded to slice it into three equal parts and lever them onto their plates.

"So, there are still good relations with Loreley, then?" Ulysse asked as he sipped, his impatience abated.

Gabriël nodded as he seated himself. "They have traded with the Lenape before we missionaries ever arrived."

"That was – what? – forty years ago?" Ulysse asked. "Cloud Village has come a long way since then, to judge by their civility."

"They owe that to our past missionaries, Pastor Schraal especially. He did not come only to preach, but to instruct the Lenape in practical things. Him, and his wife Rosamund, too."

"I seem to remember her – before I left Loreley twenty years ago," Ulysse mused. "A very pleasant and gracious lady. But you say she died ten years ago?"

Gabriël's face fell. "Not just died. Killed…"

"By?" Athenor paused the mug at his lips.

"The Winter Ghosts." Gabriël's voice was sad. "But she was not alone and or on the plain. It happened at Mountain Stream, amid other women of the village. She was helping her handmaiden wheelbarrow their water cask back home."

"My sympathies," Athenor said gently. "You must have been close with her."

"All of the village was. She was loved by us all. Pastor Schraal never recovered from his grief."

"What did the witnesses see?" Ulysse interjected.

Gabriël took a deep breath before replying. "It was not snowing, it was March, with only the last residue of ice. Other women were there with their water casks. Their talk was gradually interrupted by loud, wordless, whispering voices

– No, that isn't quite right. How can whispers be loud? But they were – like a chorus of winds singing words that no one understood.

"Then, before any of them could flee, two white whirlwinds the size of men suddenly appeared from nowhere and wrapped around Rosamund and her handmaiden, one to each. The others could see them clutch their throats as if choking. Some ran to get help. At least one picked up a rock and threw it at one of the whirlwinds, but it just glanced off and spun away.

"Mercifully, their end was short. Only a minute or two, and then the whirlwinds slowed and vanished, leaving behind two lifeless bodies…" Gabriël looked down at his mug somberly.

"Most sad," Ulysse offered perfunctorily. Sensitivity was not part of his makeup. "But also most unusual, wasn't it? I had heard the ghosts only struck in winter and only upon solitary victims."

"Not always, it seems." Gabriel shoved his mug across the table angrily. "And I heard about some recent deaths of folk from Loreley. A couple traveling together and some old woman in her attic in the middle of town."

"We have heard the same," Athenor said with a frown. "It seems these ghosts have gotten bolder over the years. Tell me, Gabriël, how long ago did the ghosts first appear?"

"As far back as any of the Lenape here remember – even Cholena – even before the first German or Dutch settler came to this area. I have no idea where they come from or why they choose to remain here. But Pastor Schraal probably knows more about them than anyone. Ever since they killed Rosamund…well, I think that it was why he spoke with Cholena so much."

"Does he still talk with her?" Athenor asked.

"Not so much anymore. I believe he feels he has learned all he can from her or perhaps…" the deacon thought for a moment, "all that she is willing to tell him."

"Have they become estranged, do you think?"

The deacon hesitated, then inclined his chin a fraction. "I think so. The last time they spoke – through Hans – was maybe a year ago. It did not end well. Cholena became agitated, which bled over to Hans, who yelled at Pastor Schraal and waved his left arm wildly. I thought that – for the first time in his life – Hans would visit violence upon someone. Since then, our pastor has not returned to this house."

"Did you ever learn what upset Cholena and Hans?"

"No. But I know that ever since Rosamund's death, Nikolasz has been a changed man. He broods and has become solitary. I now perform almost all the church services and outreach to our congregation. He seems to spend most of his time sending off buckets of money for any old books and manuscripts he can find to learn more about the Winter Ghosts, and…how they might be destroyed."

"*If* they can be destroyed," Ulysse muttered sourly. "But that is why we," he gestured at himself and Athenor, "are here. To help do that."

Gabriël's face brightened. He turned to Athenor. "That's why your name seemed familiar. I've heard about you. You've fought evil creatures in the past."

"Not alone," Athenor replied with embarrassment. "True, I have faced ghosts before, but they are notoriously hard to destroy. Usually, they can only be contained or expelled. And I must confess that I know little about your Winter Ghosts. Perhaps Pastor Schraal will share his knowledge and we can join forces to defeat them."

Gabriël's smile faded. "You can ask him, but he keeps his own counsel. When I've tried to pry, I got the impression he has some scheme in mind but fears my disapproval. Perhaps that was what caused his falling out with Chelona. I don't know."

Athenor digested that with disquietude. The only conceivable reason for such disapproval must be that the scheme involved a substantial risk of harm — and likely not to Schraal alone.

4. The Storm

They could hear the tinker's wagon before it came into sight from around a tree-crowded bend. The clatter of pots and pans proclaimed it to be no one else. Yet, naturally wary, Athenor laid a hand upon the butt of his Hawkins flintlock pistol. On his horse alongside, Ulysse hesitated, then followed his example with his Prussian horse pistol.

Thus far, they had not encountered anyone on Hop-Toad Road after leaving Cloud Village. They had seen no canoes or boats on the Paradise River that paralleled the road. Nothing was stirring in the thickets of oak and chestnut that surrounded the road and the river.

The dark cloudbank they had glimpsed yesterday had now inched across the entire sky but was still thickest above the West Wind Mountains. Although the clouds were mostly a slowly mantling black and gray, there was an odd greenish tint that suffused their undersurfaces. Flickers of lightning jabbed amid them and from across the open plain beyond the river, there came the distant mutter of thunder.

Athenor rose in his stirrups and squinted at the gathering storm and saw a gray rainy mist sweeping the plain. The rain had not reached their position yet, but the air was heavy with moisture.

"Maybe we should have stayed in Cloud Village," Ulysse grumbled, half to himself.

"Pastor Schraal made it clear his hospitality was at an end," Athenor said dryly, "and made it equally clear he would give us neither information nor help with the ghosts."

Ulysse spat out a curse. "Not to mention saying he didn't want or need our help either. What's that about?"

Athenor remembered their meeting with the pastor that morning. After breakfasting with Gabriël and Hans, they had gone to the East Wind Reformed Church in *Kùmbòhunk* where Schraal was still in his parsonage, seated at his desk. He had not been pleased to see them and suggested they had overstayed their welcome. When they broached the subject of the Winter Ghosts and their intention to help destroy them, he assured them he already had plans to do so. They had not been able to get anything more from him, but Athenor had looked down at the iron-bound books spread out on the desk. He saw that their pages were filled with blackletter Latin along with woodcut pictures of demons. When Schraal noticed his glance, he had slammed the books shut and had bidden the two a surly "Good Day."

"Whatever his plan, he bears watching," Athenor replied grimly.

Now, from around the bend they could hear a man singing in Dutch, which neither of them understood except for *Verdomme Elsje* – "Damned Elsie" – and the refrain, "Oh, tra-la, tra-la. tra-la…"

"It's a tinker, right enough," grunted Ulysse, letting his fingers slip from his pistol. "Can't say a whole sentence without adding an imprecation."[14]

Athenor drew rein but did not remove his hand from the Hawkins. Ulysse stopped beside him.

At length, the tinker's wagon came into sight, drawn by a single puffing horse. It was of four wheels, with a wooden frame covered by travel-stained canvas. Along the upper side rails were the dangling ironmongery of pots, pans, spades, and pickaxes they had heard. The tinker himself was bundled in a plain cloak and slouch hat, and when he saw them, his song trailed off and he produced what he must have thought was a winning smile. To Athenor's amused eye, it resembled a death rictus.

"Ho, noble sirs!" the tinker called out cheerfully. "How are you on this *schijt* of a day?" Not waiting for a reply, he continued, "Are you need of buying a pot or two? Or maybe sharpening your knives?" He gestured at Athenor's left leg, where the leather sheath of his scramasax dangled.

"Thank you, no," Athenor's hand relaxed. "We are bound for Loreley Town and…" he rose in his stirrups to examine the western sky, "hope to arrive before that storm reaches us."

The tinker knuckled his forehead with grudging acknowledgment. "As you say, sir. I'm off for Cloud Village

---

[14] Tinkers in those days were infamous for swearing, possibly because they frequently burned their hands when using hot solder to mend pots and pans and developed the habit. The dam of solder was sometimes shoddily applied and easily dislodged, rendering the repair useless - hence the phrase, "Not worth a tinker's dam."

myself. But I'll be back in town in a few days if you need me then. Kikkert's the name."

"*Mijnheer* Kikkert," Athenor inclined his head.

"Aren't you afraid of traveling the road alone?" interjected Ulysse impatiently.

"Oh, the legends," the tinker chuckled. "It's only in the winter months that lone travelers need beware. Although even now, I'd still not visit the ruined lodge…" He pointed behind them toward their left, where the forest mantled the foothills. They followed his gaze to see a side road not far away that led into the trees. They had noted that when they had passed it by but had given it no thought.

"It's still a fair distance to the Lenape village for you," Athenor cautioned. "If that storm comes up suddenly, we might all have to shelter there for a while."

Kikkert shrugged. "You two might, but not I, sir." Realizing there was no business to be had with these two, the tinker decided it was time to move on. He snapped his reins and the horse snorted and the wagon began trundling off again.

Athenor and Ulysse edged their horses aside for him. They spared a moment to watch him proceed behind them, then continued forward.

"Do you suppose he hasn't heard about the old charwoman in town?" Ulysse asked. "The one Oreste said was killed *after* the snows had departed?"

"Probably not. Which makes our present journey to town somewhat risky, even though we are two."

They fell into silence and their horses clip-clopped down the dusty road. Winds began to gust, kicking up dirt from the road and blowing their clothes. They peered westward in time to see stalks of lightning dart to the ground from the slow-moving scud, along with the crash of ever-nearing thunder.

They turned to look behind at a chortling laugh and saw that the ironmongery on the tinker's wagon gleamed with bluish shuddering lights. Far from being alarmed, the tinker seemed elated, throwing up his arms and shouting gusts of laughter at the sky.

"Saint Elmo's fire," Athenor shouted, above the noise of the wind. "That tinker is in line for a lightning strike."

"He must be mad to laugh that way!" Ulysse yelled, gathering his cloak tighter about him.

Rain started to fall, light at first and then increasingly heavy. And now above the noise of the wind and the rain, they heard something like a thundering waterfall. Squinting through the downpour, they saw the black wall of clouds to the west of the river begin to churn, and a vivid white funnel began to lower. The thin finger of the tornado inched down to touch the ground not three-hundred yards away to their northwest.

They paused their horses to inspect it with interest as its tip churned up a cloud of water vapor as it crossed the river and headed east. Small trees and green underbrush were torn up and swirled off while larger trees bent in the blast. Yet the mouth of the funnel seemed impossibly small, less than twenty feet in diameter.

The tornado seemed to pause in place, then began to move again while lightning streaked above it and its voice rose to a deafening bellow.

Ulysse cried out. "It's moving this way! That's impossible!"

Athenor shared his friend's surprise. He knew that tornados always moved in a southwest-to-northeast direction due to their counterclockwise rotation. But despite that, this one was moving northwest to southeast in their direction — and the direction of the tinker's wagon.

As if it was pursuing him.

That wagon was now hurtling away into the side road leading into the woods, and they could see the tinker frantically whipping his horse. Kikkert no longer laughed but was shrieking with fright. He kept looking back over his shoulder at the tornado following him, while his ironware rattled, still with a bluish-purple, fluttering luminescence. Yet, he seemed to be outdistancing the approaching cone when something rushed out of the woods along the path toward him.

They were like miniature tornados, but untethered to the clouds. Each was a vortex of feverish energy, flying a few feet off the ground. From them came a commingled chorus of sighs and wordless whispers that could be heard above the storm. Like the tornado, they were a lurid white, and in their centers, there were long, dark nuclei that also rapidly vibrated.

Within a moment, they enveloped the wagon, which began to violently rock and shudder. Kikkert tried to dive inside under the canvas cover. But before he could, he was plucked out by the feet and suspended in mid-air. All around him were those vortexes, while the wagon rattled and shook, and the horse reared and tried to rip loose from its harness.

As Athenor and Ulysse watched in horror, Kikkert was held frozen in the air, swaddled by several ghosts. They also saw the whipping tip of the tornado edge nearer the wagon, causing it to lift and shake even more fiercely.

Kikkert's scream ebbed into a prolonged exhalation, and he was precipitously dropped by the whirling ghosts back onto the wagon to lay still and broken. By this time, the horse had ripped its harness loose and was fleeing at full speed up the road.

The vortexes began to swirl away from the approaching tornado, racing for shelter in the woods. They dashed back along the side road toward the trees.

But the last one was not quick enough. The tip of the tornado lifted from the ground and lashed out like a striking snake, seizing the ghost, and holding it fast. The nearby wagon exploded to flinders, and a cloud of ironware and broken wood danced in the air.

Athenor and Ulysse could hear an eerie keening cry from the captured ghost, that rapidly receded higher and higher into the air and finally dwindled amid the black and greenish clouds. The rest of the whirlwinds disappeared into the woods, and their wordless murmurs shrank and faded away.

The tornado seemed to hesitate, while the wagon debris swirled rapidly around it. Then, it moved to follow down the side road to pause at the entrance to the woods, where it hovered for a moment. Behind it, the remnants of the wagon precipitously dropped to the ground, where they continued to swirl in the dust as if deliberately rejected by the tornado. The scattered ironware continued to glow blue. The body of Kikkert lay face down in the wet dirt.

The white cylinder then slowly turned back along the path and again hesitated, and Athenor could feel its deliberate attention – the attention of a living, intelligent creature. Then, it twisted away across the river back the way it came. The roar of its winds diminished, and the rain slackened. At length, it began to slowly retract into the churning clouds with a final echo of thunder.

Athenor and Ulysse continued to soothe their alarmed horses and then cautiously trotted toward the remains of the wagon and Kikkert. They dismounted and approached the body. Athenor knelt and turned it over.

There was no expression on the dead face – neither horror nor agony. The eyes were closed, and the mouth hung slightly open. But the skin was all ashen and blue, especially the lips. The rest of the body seemed flaccid, as if from muscular wasting. The fingernails were also blue. There was no blood or visible wound. The clothing was disheveled but not torn or ripped away.

Athenor nodded to himself. Ulysse scowled down at the body.

"Can you tell how he died?" he rasped.

"I've seen others die like this," Athenor answered quietly. "Those with lung failure, where the body has been starved of the air that normally suffuses its tissues." He lifted his palm to Ulysse. "Do you still have your Barlow knife?"

"I haven't yet thrown it away from embarrassment, if that's what you mean," Ulysse rasped, producing the small penknife from a vest pocket, and handing it over.

Athenor unfolded the blade and uncovered one of Kikkert's wrists. He carefully made a deep slash across the radial artery. Ulysse bent close to peer at the incision.

"Devil blast me!" he muttered, "That's the kind of blood that oozes from a long-dead body."

Instead of bright red, the color of the blood seeping from the incision was a dark purple. Athenor wiped the blade on the hem of Kikkert's coat, refolded the knife, and handed it back.

"Yes. After a few hours, the blood of a dead body will turn that color," he said quietly. "The air of life no longer infuses it."

"As if the breath of life was stolen from him all of a sudden," Ulysse concluded, echoing his brother's words in Leichtenberg.

Athenor rose and peered about. He spied the tinker's horse wandering near the treeline. "Friend Ulysse, can you remount and see if you can retrieve that horse? I'd prefer to take Kikkert back to town rather than bury him out here."

Ulysse noticed that the storm seemed to be subsiding. The sky was still filled with black clouds, but the greenish tinge had dissipated and there was only a drizzle of rain. He nodded glumly and went to his horse. He turned back for a moment.

"What are you going to do?"

Athenor went to his horse and swung up into the saddle. "I have a mind to see what lies down this side road."

Ulysse looked at him as if he were deranged. He began to say something, but then shrugged and cantered away toward the tinker's horse.

Athenor gave his horse a reassuring pat, then proceeded down the path. Apart from the whisper of the rain, there was only silence. He entered the woods and followed along between the damp pines and oaks. His hand automatically was at the hilt of his long-knife, although reason told him it would be useless against the ghosts.

While he rode, he pondered what he had seen.

So, those were the Winter Ghosts – sentient beings. If not made from wind, at least clothed in it.

He had glimpsed perhaps a half-dozen of them thronging about Kikkert and the wagon. Now, one of them was gone, siphoned up by the tornado, apparently to its destruction or imprisonment in the clouds.

And what to make of the tornado? Apparently, another sentient being. He recalled hearing from other Lenape tribes about what they called *Pèthakhue* or "thunder spirits," that lived in the sky and caused storms. They were said to be dangerous and at times killed people, but at other times rescued them on a whim. This tornado-being had not been in time to save Kikkert but seemingly had avenged him. Clearly, it was adversarial to the Winter Ghosts, but why?

He was still musing about this when the path debouched into a glade ringed by tall pine and slender white beech. He drew rein on his horse to stare at a two-story rectangular building made of white stone, with a cupola looming atop its flat roof and solemn windows flanking the brown front door.

Then, the structure was enveloped in blurry shimmers like a mirage and abruptly vanished. He wiped at his eyes and when he blinked them open, he saw that the structure had been replaced by ruins. The crumbling remnants of a rectangular stone foundation lay amid puddles of rainwater, wet weeds along its edge tingling with the drizzle. A broken chimney tottered up against the black swirling clouds. Jagged parts of the back wall clawed up whitely against the green wall of trees behind it.

Now he could hear a faint susurration from the ruins that began to slowly swell, and he could feel a mild rush in the air around him. His horse began to snort and paw nervously at the wet ground.

And the disquieting thought struck him:

It's not merely the house of the Winter Ghosts — but a ghost itself.

Needing no further urging, Athenor turned the horse and galloped back down the path. Behind him, the whispers faded, and then there was only the soft tap of the rain upon the stone ruins.

5. The Garret

By the time they reached the third floor, Baldur was panting and gasping and had to be helped to a sitting position in the hallway. With his wife Bella supporting one arm, and Oreste the other, they carefully guided him to the floor while he tossed his cane down. There was gray light thrown across them from the window at the far end of the corridor. Outside, rain pelted the leaded glass while the wind made it shudder.

"Don't worry, Baldur," Oreste smiled crookedly, "the way back down is easier."

"My thanks, Oreste. Even with Bella's help, I don't think I could have climbed this far." He turned to his wife, whose expression was stolid, as usual. "Don't you agree, *Liebchen?*"

"Hmm," was her only reply. Oreste inspected her from the corner of his eye. Ever since he had met them at the entrance to the boarding house, he had sensed her resentment. He supposed it to be from pride – her belief that her husband needed only *her* help. "Do you want to rest here while I and – him – search Gertrude's room?"

"No," Baldur said firmly. "As I told Oreste," he shared a glance with him, "I want to pray for Gertrude's repose as well as search for any clues about her death."

Oreste smiled indulgently. "You never fail to surprise me, my friend. Here I thought that the Reformed Church never prayed for their dead – considering it useless since they're already gone to their predestined reward…or punishment."

"Scripture doesn't forbid it," Baldur smiled. "I've read 2 Timothy and Paul's prayer about dead Onesiphorus - that the Lord grant him mercy on the day of judgment. If his fate was already determined, why bother to pray for him after death?"

"Or pray for him when he was alive," Oreste winked. "Well, I see that our talks have softened your…blessed (he was about to use a different word) …Calvinism somewhat. But don't worry, I won't betray you to your Assembly."

"If the both of you are finished, let's proceed," Bella snapped and began to lift Baldur under his shoulder. He reached for his cane but only grasped it for a moment before it fell to the floor.

Wordlessly, Oreste stooped to retrieve it. But then, at his side, he sensed Baldur wobbling, and he leaped up to steady him as he tottered at the edge of the steps. Baldur's face was blanched and there was fear in his eyes. At his shoulder, Bella's face was expressionless, and she tightened her grip on his arm. Oreste glared at her but said no rebuke for her seeming carelessness.

She met his gaze coolly and replied evenly, "There's no need for alarm, Oreste. I had him."

"These damnable buckle-shoes!" The unwonted oath betrayed Baldur's momentary distress. "Soles as slick as glass! I'll never understand why men of this day and age are supposed to wear these silly knee-breeches, long stockings, and impractical shoes! Along with these foolish tricorn hats that protect a man's head from neither sun nor rain!"

"It's expected of a gentleman, *Liebling*," Bella said smoothly, "especially one of God's anointed ministers. You can't go around wearing trousers like a sailor or a frontiersman. Or a slouch hat like a wayfarer."

Oreste was hardly listening to her words, feeling relief that his friend had just been saved from what would have been a calamitous injury. Yet, part of his mind noted that Bella did not seem to share his relief. But it was always hard to tell with her, as emotionally undemonstrative as she seemed to be. Once again, he found himself wondering why Baldur had ever married her.

Oreste handed Baldur back his cane and put his hand under his other elbow. They escorted him to the end of the hall where a final flight of low steps led up to a closed wooden door. It was secured by an iron padlock, and they paused while Bella fished inside her apron pocket and produced a key.

"Has anyone been here since the police?" Oreste asked as Bella unlocked the door and swung it forward.

"Dr. Kitzler was with them, of course," Baldur replied as his wife led him inside the room. "After Gertrude's body was removed, they locked her door. Since I was her pastor, they gave me the key, in case I wanted something of her belongings…She had no kin."

"Did you know her well?" Oreste had to relinquish Baldur's elbow to let him pass through the narrow doorway.

"Yes, fairly well. But," Baldur stopped in the doorway to turn and face Oreste, "might I ask you to wait outside for a bit? I want a few minutes alone with Bella for my prayers."

"I thought you wanted my help to search for clues." Oreste's brow wrinkled.

"More to help him up and down the stairs," Bella interjected, her eyes narrowing. "I couldn't do it alone."

Embarrassed by his wife's bluntness, Baldur smiled sheepishly at his friend and gently shut the door in his face. Oreste scowled but went back down to the hallway, sullenly shoving his hands inside his coat.

Inside the room, Baldur looked around. It was as dismal as he remembered it. A small cot-like bed with a straw mattress and a plain woolen blanket, a washstand with a water jug, a stiff wooden chair, a second-hand wardrobe, and a small hinged larder. There was only one window, against which the rain pattered. In one corner stood a cast-iron potbelly stove with a pitiful stack of firewood beside it. The door to the firebox was ajar. There was a short, stiff brush beneath the ashpan. The slightly crooked stovepipe pierced the slanting ceiling. There was a wooden trash box in the nearby corner.

"We must be quick, wife," Baldur whispered. "Oreste will start to wonder after ten or fifteen minutes."

"I don't know why you wouldn't let me come alone," Bella hissed, her previously impassive face now livid with anger. "You've described the thing to me enough times! Don't you trust me?"

"Of course, of course." He maneuvered to the bed and clumsily seated himself. "But the gem could be dangerous. It might have a defensive spell on it. And, as you said, I'm an anointed minister and likely have more spiritual protection than you." But all of that was not so. Truth be told — he did not trust her.

"Hmph!" She began searching the room, underneath the bed, inside the larder, and under the woodpile. "How do you know that drawing of it that Schraal showed you was accurate? You don't trust him, do you?"

"No. But I trusted Gertrude."

"Do you even know for certain if she found it?" She opened the gate to the firebox and peered inside. She then slid out the ashpan and ran her fingers through the accumulated soot, then paused. She withdrew her hand and wiped it on her apron next to a pocket. Her attention was then caught by something in the low trash box.

"No, I don't know for sure. She searched off and on for weeks in the Town Hall cellar — even searched the ruins after the place burned down. But she said all she found were some old animal bones."

"Like this one?" Bella fished inside the trash box and withdrew what appeared to be part of a fish or reptile skull. Most of the head was missing and only one circular orbit remained. That and the upper jaw of a very long snout. The undersurface of it was lined with remnants of hook-like teeth. She held it up distastefully for Baldur's inspection.

"Looks like an alligator gar to me," he suggested cautiously.

"What would that be doing in the foundation?"

"That foundation was close to the river. Perhaps at one time, there was a nest of them before the foundation was built."

"And this thing hasn't crumbled to dust by now?" She reluctantly ran her fingers over it. "Hmm. It feels more like stone than bone."

"Then you've answered your own question. It's been petrified over the decades."

"Is it worth anything?" She held it up for inspection.

"I don't think so. Who would want it? Gertrude must have taken it as a curiosity."

Bella disdainfully dropped it back into the box. "Even she didn't want it in the end, it seems." She wiped her hands on her apron. "Do you think she was the one who set the fire?"

Baldur considered that for a moment. "Gertrude was no criminal. I never asked her to do anything like that. And – before you ask – I didn't burn it down, either."

"Exactly how much did you tell her?"

"Only enough to impress its value on her – not its properties." Baldur closed his eyes in thought. "I told her it was something important for the church. She is – was – devoted to the church."

"Oh?" Bella sneered. "So, you told her it was valuable, eh? Then, why wouldn't she keep it for herself?" She shook her head cynically. "My poor fool of a husband! You don't understand paupers very well. Or paupers in ill health with no hope of being able to work for much longer. Do you know what it would mean to such a woman to find something she could sell to a receiver?"[15]

"I hate to think you're right," Baldur said hesitantly, opening his eyes. "But if she did find it…then, yes, that could have been the reason she didn't tell me. Oh, it's all probably hopeless anyhow! I've just been desperate for something… anything that might arrest this mysterious disease of mine."

"And you think this bauble will do that?" She gazed intently at him.

"From what Schraal said – yes. It supposedly has great restorative power if one knows the incantations to evoke it. Schraal says he does." He paused to give her a timid glance. "Maybe, maybe if it works…do you think things will get better between us?"

She eyed him coldly. "What do you mean?"

"You know what I mean." He gave her a feeble smile. "Will you love me again?"

"Of course, I love you." But she avoided meeting his eyes.

His smile turned rueful. "Bella, it's my body that's failing, not my eyesight…" When she made no reply, he continued softly, "I know you've stayed with me out of duty – even before I got sick. Wife to a poor pastor in a remote town. Our life here is not one of luxury, I know."

"You've done your best," Her tone was noncommittal.

[15] What a "fence" for stolen goods was called in those times

"Be truthful, Bella. It's been a long time since you loved me, hasn't it?"

"You're quite wrong," she said flatly, not meeting his gaze. "But let's return to the matter at hand."

"All right," He dropped his eyes to the floor.

"About Schraal. You never told me the reason he wanted the gem for himself."

Baldur hesitated before answering. "He's never been straightforward about that, but I have some suspicions of my own."

"Do you want to share those with me?" She inspected him narrowly.

"No." He was still hurt by her response. "Not for the present."

She retrieved a handkerchief from a second apron pocket and wiped her sooty hand. "Well, it seems to me Gertrude failed. That gem isn't anywhere in this little garret."

She was about to say more when there came a rap at the door, and it eased open to admit Oreste's tentative face.

"Are you finished with your prayers?" he asked quietly. "Have you had a chance to search for clues yet?"

Baldur was about to respond when Bella clipped out a terse, "Yes. There's nothing."

Oreste frowned and scanned the room. "It all looks ordinary enough, in truth." He went to the window and tested it, flipping the latch and opening it a few inches to admit a blast of rain. He quickly closed and latched it again and shook the water from his hand. "I suppose she might have slept with the window open the night she was killed…" He turned his gaze to the slanting ceiling. "No leaks…How did the ghosts enter, I wonder?"

Baldur sighed and turned his head to look at a plain wooden cross nailed to the wall above the bed. "Her faith didn't shield her, did it?" He shook that thought away, and continued, "Do you suppose they can simply materialize out of thin air?"

Oreste thought for a moment. "Everything we know about them suggests otherwise. I would guess that – being made of 'spirit-stuff' – their forms are plastic and able to compress at times to ooze in and out of narrow openings."

At that, Bella blinked at the stovepipe but said nothing. Neither man noticed her reaction.

"I'm afraid we've wasted your time, friend Oreste," Baldur muttered. "There's nothing here to help us." He beckoned Bella over and she helped him to his feet, replacing the handkerchief into her apron pocket.

Oreste handed him his cane and lent his elbow another hand. Together, he and Bella guided him to the door and down the steps to the third-floor landing.

"I'll just close that door," Oreste relinquished Baldur's arm and remounted the steps. Behind him, Bella looped Baldur's arm over her shoulder to steady him, her other hand still inside her apron pocket.

Oreste took a last look around the garret, then shook his head, and closed and locked the door. He went to Baldur's other side and put his hand under his elbow. They started back carefully toward the staircase. Oreste hesitated as a sudden thought struck him.

"You know," he said, half to himself, "I think we haven't asked ourselves the most important question. Not how the ghosts entered the garret and killed Gertrude, but…*why?*"

Baldur and Bella fought an impulse to exchange a glance. But Bella's fist inside the apron pocket suddenly tightened.

6. Egon Richter

The Pastorius County Office of the Sheriff was located just east of where Town Hall used to stand and just south of the county courthouse. Like most of the structures in Loreley, it was of the traditional Bavarian-style architecture – narrow and long, with a sharply-peaked roof and black extruded beams crisscrossing a white wooden exterior. Unlike similar constabularies and shrievalties, its gaol was not in a cellar, but on the third floor. The Loreley shrievalty had less than twenty deputies – enough for a town of this size at that time. Most townsfolk were honest citizens and were more than capable of defending themselves and their families in ordinary circumstances. The most common crime was thievery, but the occasional brawling drunkard or vagrant needed a few days behind bars. At present, the eight cells were empty, and most of the deputies were on patrol or responding to requests from outlying farmsteads and cottages.

Sheriff Egon Richter rose from behind his massive desk on the first floor to stretch and idly scratch the hair on his ears. On the wall behind him, an assortment of firearms was mounted – Brown Bess and Charleville muskets, a Pennsylvania long rifle, some antique wheel-lock muskets, and even a restored Portuguese matchlock rifle chased with gold and inlaid with ivory.

The rain seemed to be ebbing, and he ambled to the front door and eased it open to lean against the side jamb. There was a low porch in front and he stepped out and turned to inspect the ruins of Town Hall.

It was still unclear if the fire that gutted it was accidental or not. There had been barrels of whale oil stored in the cellar to supply the many lamps in the building. In retrospect, it had been stupid to store the town archives – documents in folders and folios – on the dozens of shelves nearby. It did not take much for the blaze to ignite them and hopelessly spread to the ceiling and consume the upper floors.

But he could not fathom why anyone would have deliberately set the fire. The most important records in town were in the courthouse. What would anyone have to gain? But perhaps it was not a crime of calculation but of passion, such as revenge. Yet, the fire happened at night when no county employee was present. So, if that was the motive, it only produced a feeble revenge.

He stirred himself from his reverie as two men on horseback approached, leading a third horse across which a blanket-draped body hung. He turned to whistle to the lone deputy on duty behind him.

"Herbst," he called sharply. At that, a stoic man of middle height with a vulpine face and a black mustache rose from his escritoire and wandered to his side. Together, they stood in the doorway and watched as the three horses clopped near.

The two men both wore rain-dampened cloaks and wide-brimmed slouch hats. One was of average height with a serious demeanor, the other was much shorter, with a long and gloomy face. They trotted up to the long hitching rail in front of the porch and carefully swung down. While the shorter man tied up their horses, the other disengaged the reins of the third horse and led it to the railing.

"I'm afraid we've brought new business for you," he said to Richter, sensing him as the one in charge.

The sheriff nudged Herbst, and the deputy joined Athenor in lifting the body down. Together, they carried it onto the porch and into the office, as Richter stepped aside to make room. As they proceeded down the hallway to a door Herbst indicated, Ulysse came up to the sheriff and cleared his throat.

"It's still raining out here if you haven't noticed," he snapped, and Richter flinched and motioned him inside. Ulysse took off his hat, shook it out, and closed the door.

"Ulysse von Mardure," he clipped out, "Form…uh, Mayor of Dereham." There was no point in admitting he was a *former* mayor and possibly some advantage in maintaining the fiction.

"Oh?" Richter beckoned him to follow down the hall. "You're the Lutheran pastor's cousin?"

"That's right. And my companion is Dr. Seth Athenor." He unfastened his cloak and draped it over an arm, having to double it so it would not drag along the floor.

"Is he indeed?" Richter tried to mute the skepticism from his voice. "Well, we were expecting you both, but not with a corpse. What happened? Who is it?"

"A tinker. He called himself Kikkert."

"Did you two kill him?" Richter went to the door where Athenor and Herbst had gone.

"If we did, it would have been for a sound reason." Ulysse grimaced with exasperation. "But we didn't."

They entered a small room with a long table in the center and several chairs set along the paneled walls. The tinker's corpse was laid on the table, face-up, face and hands still tinted grayish blue.

Athenor had removed his hat and cloak to drape them over one of the chairs. Richter eyed him doubtfully. He was not dressed as Richter thought a doctor should. Instead of the usual city garb, he wore a dark green deerskin overshirt, buckskin trousers, and high, laced moccasins. In his pale leather belt were a long-barreled pistol and a long-knife whose sheath dangled to the knee. He looked more like a frontiersman or hunter than a physician. Athenor noticed his critical gaze and smiled thinly.

"We've traveled a long way," he said, "Through forest and bog and in bad weather…"

"All the way from Leichtenberg," finished Ulysse. "The doctor didn't come to compete in a fashion contest."

"No, no," Richter waved an apologetic hand at Athenor. "You're just different from my expectation."

"You look familiar, Sheriff," Athenor ignored the remark. "Have you ever been to the upcountry of New Hampshire? Do you have a brother or cousin who might have trapped there or in Canada, perhaps?"

For Richter reminded him of someone from when he was a French Colonial Marine – someone it now pained him to recall. A trapper and his companion had tried to rob him on a forest trail. Athenor had quickly killed the companion and wounded the trapper, who had fallen to his knees and begged for mercy. Mercy that Athenor's pistol had not granted him.

"…No, I have no relatives there. My family is all here in Loreley," Richter was replying, wondering at this line of inquiry.

"No matter." Athenor tried to shake away those guilty memories. "The issue at hand is the ghosts plaguing your town. This man," He waved a hand at Kikkert, "was killed by them. We both saw it happen."

"Did you, now?" Richter replied carefully. "And what, pray, do you think you saw?"

"We didn't dream it," Ulysse said sourly. "You're the sheriff, I assume?"

"Yes." Richter cleared his throat and lifted his chin imperiously. "I have that distinction, sir. I'm Egon Richter. And you've brought me a dead body that needs inspection as to the cause of death."

"But we've already…" Ulysse began until Athenor cut him off with a gesture.

"You mean by your local physician, I take it?" Athenor arched an eyebrow.

Richter turned to Herbst, who was idly gazing at the corpse. "Georg, will you fetch Dr. Kitzler? He's probably at the rathskeller for dinner."

Herbst knuckled his forehead and hurried into the hallway to the front door, where he took down a cloak and shako from pegs and went out into the drizzle.

"Should we wait?" Athenor began to be irritated. He sensed that the sheriff was more interested in suppressing his opinion rather than welcoming it, and likely this "Dr. Kitzler" was summoned to do just that.

"I don't think so. You're going to be staying in town for a while. I'm sure you're eager to get settled."

It was obvious the sheriff was trying to get rid of them. Athenor was not going to make it that easy. Besides, he was curious to meet the local physician and appraise him — unlikely he would be an ally, but might he prove to be neutral at least or — an enemy. It would be useful to know.

"We can wait," he answered tersely, retrieving his cloak and hat from the chair to hang from his arm. Richter looked like he was going to object, then controlled himself and wordlessly led them back into the hallway.

As they followed him, Athenor and Ulysse exchanged a knowing glance. "Don't you want to get our statements?" Ulysse said to Richter's retreating backside.

"All in good time, Mr. Von Mardure." He returned to the waiting area in front of his desk and waved them to a couple of chairs.

Ulysse winced. *So, Mr. instead of Mayor!* Had the news of his displacement already reached these parts? Despite his relief at vacating that unenviable office, the way the Dereham Town Council did it still rankled him.

He and Athenor hung their hats and cloaks near the front door. They waited in uncomfortable silence. There was a cast-iron stove in a nearby corner, that threw welcome heat. After a while, Athenor made an idle comment about the firearms on the wall, to which Richter nodded proudly, perhaps eager to relieve the tense atmosphere.

"You are interested in weaponry, Doctor? Do you know I used to be a gunsmith before becoming a deputy and eventually the sheriff here? Those are weapons I refurbished with my own hands. I used to make munitions, too – musket- and pistol-balls." He pointed to the Portuguese matchlock. "That is the pride of my collection. It belonged to a prince of Moçambique. It was quite expensive and only offered for sale to men of quality."

Like yourself? Athenor thought but did not say. *Yes, I think I have your measure now. A haughty laggard with a soft job who makes no waves nor ruffles any feathers. Someone with an interest in keeping Kikkert's murder silent – and Ulysse and I along with it.*

His thoughts were interrupted as the front door opened to admit Herbst and behind him, Dr. Athaulf Kitzler. They stomped their feet and removed their cloaks and headgear to hang alongside those of Athenor and Ulysse.

"I hope it's as important as your man said," sniffed Kiztler petulantly, glaring at Richter.

"Likely it's not, dear doctor," the sheriff purred. "But I just want the formality of your opinion on a certain corpse."

Before you close the case – 'formally.' Athenor nodded to himself. He reluctantly rose to his feet and extended his hand to Kitzler.

The town physician looked at the hand like it was a poisonous reptile, but grudgingly gave it a tepid clasp. Ulysse had also gotten up but did not offer his hand.

"Let me introduce our guests…" Richter explained who they were and what had brought them to his office. Kitzler digested that with a sour expression.

"Very well," he finally said, smoothing his pointed blond mustache. "I just hope you know, Sheriff, that you've interrupted my dinner at the rathskeller."

"Just as well," Ulysse smiled sarcastically. "You might have upchucked it after seeing the body."

"Hmph," was Kitzler's only reply, as he followed Richter and Herbst down the hall, not waiting for Ulysse and Athenor.

They all entered the small room and crowded around the table where Kikkert's body lay. Kitzler shrugged his coat off and rolled up his sleeves. Athenor lifted a quizzical eyebrow, uncertain as to the town physician's intentions. *Was he going to perform an autopsy? With no surgical instruments at hand?*

But Kitzler evidently was merely putting on a performance for the sheriff and deputy. He circled the body, poking here and there, prising open an eyelid to examine the pupil, opening the mouth to peer inside, tut-tutting now and then as if discovering significant facts. Finally, he straightened and pulled a handkerchief from his waistcoat pocket, and wiped his hands.

"Well, well," he said smoothly. "I see nothing unusual here, for a body that's likely been dead a few days out in the cold. Dead from exposure."

"But it's not been a few days!" Ulysse exclaimed indignantly. "He was killed only a few hours ago!"

"You've said that to Sheriff Richter, I understand. But I would politely suggest you only thought that's what you saw."

"What about this?" Ulysse pointed to Kikkert's wrist, where Athenor had made an incision. "Look at the color of that blood."

Kitzler leaned over and shook his head. "What's so unusual about that? It only takes a few hours for blood to turn that purple color, and this man's probably been dead for days."

"But it was that color only minutes after he died!" Ulysse shouted angrily. "Both Dr. Athenor and I saw it!"

Athenor had refrained from making any remark during that exchange, having concluded it was hopeless to reason with men who had already made up their minds. But now, he felt he had to stand up for his friend, so he quietly added, "That's correct."

Kitzler turned to him with a mocking grin. "So, you're the famous *Dr.* Athenor? I've heard much about you…"

Athenor waited for the inevitable rebuke, and it was not long in coming.

"…I've heard you're quite the warrior. Killed supernatural creatures – and people, too, I understand. Tell me, *Doctor* (he gave the title a sarcastic pronunciation), have you really murdered more people than you've treated?"

The acidic retort that had been forming died on Athenor's lips, and a wave of shame and embarrassment washed over him, remembering what had happened on that forest trail. He tried to keep from showing it, but he felt the sting of an earned rebuke like the stab of a needle.

Yes, he had killed more than just supernatural creatures in the past – the trapper was only one of many. He had had no pity or remorse for an adversary in those days. But as the trapper's agonized, pleading face swam back into his mind, he now felt the mercy he ought to have shown then – instead of coldly executing a terrified man.

So, he made no reply, momentarily deflated. Ulysse's face was somber, sensing his friend's hidden distress, not knowing what to say.

Kitzler eyed them both smugly, rolled down his sleeves, and retrieved his coat.

"I think we're done here," he said to Richter. "The facts are clear. I would suggest to you two…" his voice took on a mocking lilt, "that you try not to drink so much."

Ulysse began to bristle, but at Athenor's touch on his elbow, subsided into simmering silence.

"We'll be on our way now," Athenor said flatly, "but what should be done with Kikkert's horse?"

"We don't want to be accused of horse thievery," Ulysse said gruffly.

"Perhaps I could borrow it for the day?" came a voice from the doorway. "It would save me from splashing home through the mud."

They turned to see Oreste smiling broadly. Ulysse's face brightened, and he came forward with his hand extended. The pastor shook it, but they did not embrace. Athenor hid a smile, realizing that the reticence for expressing affection he had noted in Ulysse and Laerte extended to their cousin as well.

"Pastor," Richter blustered," how did you know your cousin was here?"

"I overheard your man Herbst while I was sipping some mulled wine at the Tatzelwürm Rathskeller." He paused to wink at Ulysse. "I waited until I finished it before starting out." Oreste turned to Athenor and shook his hand as well.

"Dr. Athenor," He inclined his head a fraction with respect. "I'm most grateful you've come. We're in need of your expertise in Loreley."

At that, Kitzler scowled but said nothing. Richter looked uncomfortable.

"But who is that?" Oreste glanced at the body on the table as he relinquished Athenor's hand. He bent close. "I know him, by gad. It's Felix Kikkert, the tinker. What happened?"

"Dead from exposure," Kitzler snapped peremptorily, "probably died a week ago."

Oreste cocked his head to scrutinize the town physician. "That can't be true. He was at my house two days ago, mending a pot for my wife Johanna." He swiveled to Athenor. "Do you concur with that, doctor?"

"Who can say?" He favored Kitzler with a sarcastic smile. "After all, Ulysse and I might have been too drunk to tell."

At that, Kitzler sniffed and strode haughtily from the room and down the hall. Mumbling an excuse, Richter followed, along with Herbst trailing after.

"What's it all about?" Oreste's face puckered with bewilderment.

"We'll explain in more…favorable surroundings, Pastor," Athenor answered.

"I was just on my way home," Oreste said. "Have you an appetite for supper? Yes? Well, I'm sure Johanna can fix us all some. You can settle in, have a smoke, and we'll talk. There's a stables near my house where I can leave poor Kikkert's horse. But first," He turned to Kikkert's body, made the sign of the cross, and began to say a prayer for him.

Hurriedly, both Athenor and Ulysse followed his example and bowed their heads in silence. But Athenor's thoughts were not so much on the prayer as on his neglect in offering one before now. Had he become so hardened to death as to forget that Kikkert had not been merely a victim, but a fellow human being?

When they finished, Ulysse proceeded impatiently out into the hall toward the front door. Oreste was about to follow when Athenor plucked at his sleeve.

"Pastor," he said quietly, "Forgive my ignorance, but do Lutheran ministers ever take private Confession? And…are they empowered to give Holy Absolution?" But he wondered if even that might not expunge his feelings of guilt.

7. Oreste and Johanna

"…and how can I call myself a physician – dedicated to preserving life – and yet unhesitatingly kill others whenever I see fit? To heal with one hand and deal death with the other?" Athenor's hushed voice tapered into silence.

Oreste, seated across from him in his study, rubbed his square chin meditatively. "I believe you are too hard on yourself, friend Seth. From what I've heard of you, including from my cousins, you are a good man – whether you believe it or not. I would also say that a physician is not merely a healer of the sick, but a guardian of human life. To do that, a doctor must fight to destroy diseases that imperil it…and I dare say that some of those diseases walk on two legs."

Athenor digested that in silence but remained unconvinced. He had long understood that he was unable to change the past. He could now only do the best he could, moving ahead into what remained of his life in this world. And to hope that, in the balance, his devotion to healing others would outweigh any necessary killings - when the time came for his judgment before the Great White Throne.

Sensing that he had finished his Confession, Oreste rose to his feet and placed his palm atop the physician's head, and began the Lutheran Prayer of Absolution, "In the stead and by the command of my Lord Jesus Christ, I forgive you all your sins…"

When he finished, he patted Athenor on the shoulder and moved to the door. "Come out when you're ready," he called back over his shoulder. "If I know him, Ulysse is likely becoming impatient for us to rejoin him — unless he's found my liquor cabinet."

He opened the door and exited into the parlor, where Athenor could hear the clatter of dishes being cleared by Oreste's wife, Johanna. Taking a breath, he got to his feet, smoothed back his hair, and went out of the study.

Ulysse was sitting at the dining table, moodily sipping a glass of rum. He glanced up as first Oreste and then Athenor joined him.

"Are you enjoying that, cousin?" Oreste smiled. "The Tatzelwürm distills it itself. It's bottled as *Todesteufel* – 'Death Devil' – I believe because one glassful is guaranteed to kill off any personal demons you have."

"Maybe we should feed it to the ghosts, then," Ulysse rasped. "Are you two finished? We want to tell you what we saw today and hear your thoughts. After that, I'm set for bed. It's been a long and hard day."

"Of course," Oreste smiled indulgently, then turned to Athenor. "Doctor, will you join us in a glass?"

"Perhaps more than one." Athenor turned to call out to Johanna, who was placing their dirty plates into a pan of soapy water. "And Frau Von Mardure, my thanks for a splendid meal. I especially enjoyed that rabbit stew — what did you call it?"

Johanna was a sturdy woman somewhere in her fifties, with a pleasant face and matching disposition. "Not at all,

Doctor. We call it *hasenpfeffer*, we braise the meat with wine and onions and slow cook it for hours."

"Might I add you're wise to use copper and bronze pans and pots? They're quite common in Europe and leave a better flavor than those made from iron."

He turned to follow Oreste and Ulysse as they retreated into the study. Once inside, he shut the door and resumed his seat while the others found theirs. The iron stove in one corner emitted a comfortable heat. Candles on the book-piled desk shed a low illumination on the hardwood floor and the spines of the many books crowding the walls.

After exchanging a glance with Ulysse, Athenor launched into an account of what happened to Kikkert that morning on Hop-Toad Road. He paused from time to time to sip his drink, while Oreste gazed at him thoughtfully, fingers tented atop the desk.

When he finished, Oreste pursued his lips. "That can only have been the Winter Ghosts, of course. The part about the tornado seeming to chase and then absorb one is something I have not heard before. It is most interesting – what you've mentioned about the Lenape myth of the thunder-beings. What did you call them?"

"*Pèthakhue.*"

"I don't think they can be considered a myth at this point," Ulysse interjected.

Oreste ignored the gibe and continued, "Tornados are not rare in these parts, of course. They are most deadly in the spring and fall and usually happen out on the plain. Thus far, we have not had one in Loreley itself, although that is certainly possible. But what is your thought, Doctor? Two types of ghost creatures – the whirlwinds and the tornado?"

"Yes. And apparently inimical to each other," Athenor replied. "Have there been any killings of people by a tornado alone?"

"Well, of course – by the usual kind. But I've not heard about tornados actively chasing after someone or going against the laws of nature by moving in any direction at will."

"How many whirlwind ghosts have ever been seen at one time, do you know?" Athenor asked.

Oreste considered for a moment. "I can't say for certain, but it seems to me that back in the old days – and I'm thinking of when I was a child – people used to say there were a dozen or more. But that many haven't been reported for years. Perhaps only a half-dozen at a time, now."

"Minus one," Ulysse drained his glass.

"I wonder," Oreste darted his cousin an exasperated glance at his meaningless interruptions. "I wonder if the reason is that, one by one, those whirlwinds have been gulped up by the tornado-being, the *Pèthakhue*, over the years. Interesting…"

"And perhaps the reason why the ghosts have hitherto appeared in winter is that snow tornados are both rare and feeble," Athenor mused. "Perhaps the whirlwinds felt more emboldened during those months, had less to fear from *Pèthakhue*."

"Then why have they started appearing now, in the spring?" Ulysse interjected. "Doing so destroyed one."

"At last, an important question, cousin!" Oreste snorted a laugh.

"Yes." Athenor did not mention he had already thought of that. *Let Ulysse have his moment.* "Something very important has made them come out now, despite the danger. But what?"

"Why do you think they used to attack only solitary travelers and leave parties of two or more alone?" Ulysse asked, still pursuing his train of thought.

"No witnesses?" Athenor shrugged. He turned to Oreste. "This elderly woman that died in town during the spring a month or so ago. Why her and not someone else, do you suppose?"

"We've been considering that question ever since she died, Baldur Rathenau and I," Oreste answered. "We even went to her attic this morning to see what clues we could find."

"And?"

"Nothing," Oreste sighed. "If she was a targeted victim and not merely a random one, I have no idea why. But Baldur knew her, and I did not. She was a member of his congregation. But – before you ask – he's already told me he doesn't know anything either."

"You've earlier said that Pastor Rathenau *does* have some knowledge of the ghosts, though? From his research?"

"Yes, but mostly from what Pastor Schraal told him…"

"Oh, we've had the dubious pleasure of his acquaintance," Ulysse groaned and proceeded to tell Oreste of their experience in Cloud Village.

Oreste contemplated that. "It comes as no surprise. The only person Schraal confided in after his wife's death was Baldur…"

"We learned about the death of Schraal's wife from his deacon…" interrupted Ulysse.

"Good, good," Oreste replied, "but then they had a falling out. Whenever Schraal comes to town, he avoids Baldur – so I've been told."

"Well, if Schraal will not speak with any of us, perhaps it would pay for me to talk with your friend Baldur," Athenor suggested.

Oreste's brow wrinkled with puzzlement. "Do you think he has been holding back something from me?"

Athenor smiled apologetically. "Not necessarily. But sometimes a different questioner will yield different answers."

"Well, if you think it worthwhile, we can visit him tomorrow. I wanted you to see him anyway – as a physician. He has been in poor health over the last year or so." Oreste went on to describe his friend's symptoms.

Athenor nodded. "Certainly, I'm glad to offer what help I can." He gave no hypothesis about possible diagnoses.

"Well, that's settled," Ulysse grunted, rising from his chair, "Thank Heaven. These old bones have been wanting sleep for the past couple of hours."

Oreste got up from behind the desk. "I'm afraid we only have one spare bed. It might be a close fit for the two of you…"

"If you've blankets, I'll be fine camping on the floor," Athenor smiled. "But…" he leaned close to Oreste's ear to whisper, "I'd appreciate the loan of some cotton for my ears…I'm afraid your cousin snores badly."

Ulysse overheard him. "Add an extra pair of wads for me," he grumbled but then winked at Athenor. "Sometimes, I even wake myself up."

Oreste opened the door and led them out of the study. Johanna met him at the foot of the stairs, with blankets in her arms, hesitating between Athenor and Ulysse. Athenor smiled at her and accepted them. Ulysse had already started up the stairs where a candle in a sconce illuminated the second-floor hallway.

"Last door," Johanna called up to him.

"He might fall asleep before he reaches it," Athenor joked. "But my thanks once again for your hospitality, *Frau Von Mardure*."

She patted his arm. "Johanna. It was our pleasure, Oreste's and mine."

He gave them both a smile and turned to ascend the stairs.

Oreste and Johanna watched them go, holding each other about the waist. "I like Seth. I'm glad he's here to help us."

"And Ulysse?" Oreste winked.

"An example of the traditional Von Mardure grumpiness," she grinned indulgently. "Only in your case, it's but a thin veneer to hide your heart…The best of hearts."

He gave her a squeeze. "Well, if I've got a good heart, it's because of your influence, *Liebling*. But I'm glad the doctor is here, as well. Not just for the ghosts, but to help Baldur."

Her face turned somber. "I know. I'm worried about him, too. He's getting worse, despite Dr. Kitzler's treatment."

"Or lack of it. At least he has Bella to help him."

"Bella!" She snorted. "Yes, she puts on a good show that she cares for her husband, but…"

"But?"

"A woman can see through another woman, where a man cannot." She turned to lock eyes with him solemnly. "I don't believe she loves Baldur at all. Leaving him in her care is like leaving a puppy in the coils of a snake."

8. Athaulf Kitzler

The sunrise had barely reddened the eastern rooftops when Bella Rathenau quietly crept out her front door and carefully shut it behind her. It had stopped raining but it was still chilly enough for her to gather her shawl tighter and put her hands into the pockets of her apron. One hand idly fingered the object within one of them.

There was no one else out in the vicinity of their parsonage and the adjacent Reformed Church building. The white wooden belltower threw its long shadow down onto the grass-bordered dirt lane. To the south, the skeletal ruins of Town Hall held their own murk fast inside.

Her destination was not far – a long, low building with the typical white exterior and extruded network of black beams. Yellow lamplight burned in one of the windows bracketing the front door. Above the entrance was a plaque emblazoned with the familiar Staff of Aesculapius – a single serpent entwined about a vertical rod. If that were not enough to identify it, below that was a title painted in German Gothic - *Mediclin Klinik von Herr Dr. Kitzler.*

She opened the door – it was never locked; a nurse was always on duty – and stepped into the waiting area. There were plain wooden chairs without fabric covers (blood was too difficult to wash out) and a chest-high open window next to the door leading back. From the window came the drone of someone snoring. She smirked, guessing who it was. She went and knocked sharply on the counter in front of the window.

A sandy-haired man in his mid-thirties snorted awake in his chair and pawed at his eyes. "Oh," he mumbled, "it's you, *Frau* Rathenau…"

"And good morning to you, Alistair," she replied haughtily. "Is the doctor in?"

Alistair Nathan straightened in his chair and fumbled himself awake. "He's just arrived, *Gnädige Frau*. Please go back to his office." He waved a hand at the nearby door.

Without another word, she let herself in and proceeded down the hallway toward a sturdy door at the end and quietly knocked and entered.

Nathan watched her go, admiring her figure from the rear and hiding a grin. Like some of the other nurses[16] at the clinic, he had suspicions about her and Dr. Kitzler but knew better than to gossip about them. In his case, he had no wish to jeopardize his position — it had been hard enough to find after the destruction of Fort Saint Michael in Droitwijk in 1752. He had worked in the fort's infirmary under Nigel Varney, but after that doctor was named to head the new Martyrs' Memorial Hospital, his application was rejected.[17] Nor could he get a favorable recommendation from Dr. Varney for anywhere else.

But he had now worked under Dr. Kitzler for two years, and found him to be an appreciative employer, leaving much of the medical work to the nurses and midwives. The clinic

---

[16] The title and profession of nursing dates to at least the late Roman Empire, which built a network of hospitals staffed with both physicians and nurses. At the time of this story, nurses were almost exclusively men.

[17] As related in *The Cellar in Ghost Hill*

had been existent for fifteen years, and Dr. Kitzler himself was an accomplished physician and surgeon who had built an enviable professional reputation among the town's leading citizens. His personal reputation was that of a *bon vivant*, and ladies' man, although never seriously linked with any particular lady. Or so it was believed.

"…and where did you find it, again?" Kitzler drew his lips back from Bella's.

She exhaled and unwrapped her arms from around his neck. His kiss left a smile on her lips, and she slowly opened her eyes.

"It's been so long, my love," she whispered, ignoring his question. "I hate having to sneak and hide."

He released his embrace and smoothed back his hair. "It shouldn't be much longer, I think. Then, after a suitable period of mourning, we can announce our engagement."

"I can wait a little longer, I guess," she frowned. "But I find it hard to pretend to be the loving wife to that…that weakling Baldur."

He grinned and leaned against his neat and orderly desk, where a candelabra threw light around the book-lined walls. Between the bookshelves were pillars with bronze and silver statuettes depicting various wild animals – bears, panthers, lions, wolves. On the wall behind the desk was hung a large, framed diploma made of sheepskin, with traditional German Gothic letters:

UNIVERSETEIT LEIDEN

Faculteit Geneeskunde

Bachelor in de Wetenschappen

Kitzler had no false modesty about his medical education at that prestigious university in the Netherlands. Most townsfolk were suitably impressed by his credentials and acknowledged his medical expertise. Only the most discerning would occasionally wonder why someone with so distinguished a pedigree would choose to live in a modest town far from a cultural center like Philadelphia or New York City, much less the cosmopolitan cities of Europe. And even fewer still speculated that the good doctor had run away from some kind of scandal. But considering the sway he had with local officials in Loreley, none of these dared voice their speculation publicly.

"I assume he's been too weak to expect any romance from you, at least?" Baldur replied.

"Yes, thank Heaven!" she laughed. "It was getting harder and harder for me to pretend. Not that Baldur was ever the kind of lover you are. He's so tiny…" Her voice dripped with scorn.

He joined her laughter, then hushed himself, waving a hand toward the door. "We should be quieter. Nathan might overhear…Now, let me see it again."

She reached inside her apron pocket and fished out a palm-sized dull black gem. It was set in a rectangular iron mounting, etched with arcane glyphs. She handed it to him, and he bent close to inspect it.

"So this is the *Oculus Velnias*…The Eye of Velnias… What does it mean?"

"I don't know for sure. Baldur never shared much about the history of the gem. Only that it dates to ancient Roman times or maybe even earlier. He says it somehow wound up being buried in the foundation of Town Hall."

"The foundation that was already here when the first German settlers arrived." Kitzler held up the gem to the candlelight. "How did Baldur know that?"

"Nikolasz Schraal." Bella's voice unconsciously lowered. "He knows all about it. He was searching for it, too, and enlisted Baldur to help. He's been searching for years and somehow learned it had been secreted in the foundation."

"By whom, I wonder? Whoever built that foundation and whatever building once sat atop it, I would surmise." Kitzler turned the gem in the candlelight. "And you say the charwoman was the one who found it?"

"Yes. Gertrude Vogt. Baldur enlisted her to search Town Hall even before it burned down. He wasn't sure she had found it, but I believed she had." Bella said scornfully. "I thought she kept it for herself to sell to a receiver. Fortunately for us, she died before she could do that. Baldur and I searched her room yesterday and I found it hidden in the ashpan of her stove."

"Does Baldur know?"

"Of course not! Do I look like a fool to you? Only you and I know."

"But he genuinely thinks the gem has some kind of restorative power?"

"That's what Schraal told him. But only if the correct incantations are said – and Schraal hasn't shared those. He promised Baldur if he found the gem, he would."

Kitzler rubbed his chin thoughtfully. "I wonder. But he'd be unlikely to share them with us, for sure. So, the thing is of no use to me in treating patients. Too bad, I could have made a fortune off it, charging the sick whatever price I wanted." He smiled at the thought.

She thought for a moment. "Even if it doesn't heal anyone, you could claim that it does. Haven't supposed cures been peddled before – worthless, but desperate fools bought them anyway?"

"I only have the one gem. I can't sell it to a hundred hypochondriacs.[18] But I might just be able to sell it to one patient…One very rich patient who might buy it as a religious remedy that will heal him, if combined with fervent prayers."

"What happens when it has no effect?"

Kitzler shrugged. "I'll tell him he hasn't been praying hard enough."

She sighed and returned to his arms. "I don't know. I've begun to doubt whether anything Schraal told Baldur was true. I think he held out the promise of a cure just to encourage Baldur to find it for him."

Kitzler smiled. "You might be right. And how exactly does the pastor of a pismire church in an Indian village know anything at all about it, let alone about mystical incantations?"

---

[18] The term came into medical usage in the 1600s.

"It seems you weren't the only person educated on the Continent. Schraal attended Heidelberg University and studied history and philosophy before turning to the clergy."

Kitzler snorted. "And he gave all that up to come here? What was he running away from?"

She smiled mischievously. "Maybe the same thing as you, my dear one."

Kitzler's mouth twisted as if he had bitten something sour. He silently cursed himself for ever letting her know about his past as a newly minted physician in Rotterdam, when he had seduced some of his young female patients with small doses of "Devil's Trumpets"[19] – an aphrodisiac and deliriant – and how the ensuing scandal forced him to flee to the New World.

He retrieved a small velvet sack from a drawer and slipped the gem inside. "Well, if I can't use it to 'heal' an unending stream of patients, then we'll have to sell it to get some profit from it. I suppose we could sell it to a receiver ourselves, but it might be worth much more to Schraal."

"I think so, too. He'll likely pay a good price for it." Bella went over to touch Kitzler's elbow. "I understand he has some family money."

"Hmm." Kitzler raised a skeptical eyebrow. "According to whom? Him? If that's true, you'd never know it from the way he lives. In a miserable hut in a miserable Native village."

____

[19] Aka Jimson Weed, which grew in both Europe and North America.

"But Schraal wants the gem badly! That's why he enlisted Baldur's help, to begin with. Baldur says he thinks it will help raise his wife from the dead. At least, that's what he said."

"And Baldur believes that? And that if he found the gem, Schraal would truly help cure him of his *mysterious illness?*" He said the last with a mocking lilt.

"With any luck, he won't get a chance to try!" She threw her arms around his waist and tilted her chin to gaze up at him. "How much longer before that poison finishes its work?"

"A few more months," he replied coolly. "It takes a while for lead poisoning to kill someone. Are you feeding it to him with every meal now?"

"Yes, I mix the dust into his favorite sauerkraut soup and *schinkennudeln.*[20] I hide the taste with seasonings and sauces. We also use iron cookware, like most folk. So, whenever he complains of a metal taste, I just remind him of that."

"Lead powder is so easy to procure," he sniggered. "One has only to grind down musket-balls, for instance. You only must be careful by using small, repeated doses – not only to hide the taste but to produce a slow poisoning effect."

"So, you will take the gem to Schraal?" Her eyes were bright with joy.

He shook his head. "I'll send a message with Nathan to Cloud Village for him to come here to town. I don't think it's safe to meet him on his home ground."

---

[20] German ham and cheese noodle casserole

"Safety, yes…" Her eyes fell with a somber thought. "Do you know that Baldur thinks the ghosts killed Gertrude for the gem?"

"Ha! The ghosts?" he smiled thinly. "Do *you* believe that twaddle?"

"I believe what you believe, *Liebchen*. Still…maybe you shouldn't hold onto the gem any longer than necessary."

"Perhaps you're right." But his gaze drifted over her head as he gave thought to a different idea.

9. Baldur Rathenau

"By the by, Oreste," Athenor splashed through the still-drying muddy street alongside the pastor, "what do you know of that ruined house on Hop-Toad Road?" He shifted the medical satchel hanging from his shoulder.

"No more than anyone." The pastor looked to his other side, where Ulysse was trudging. "What about you, cousin?"

"I left Loreley when little more than a youth. All I know is children's tales. 'Beware of the White Lodge.' Travelers enter but never come back out. That sort of thing." Ulysse paused to prod his memory. "You remember, cousin. That time when you and I – and Laerte – went to see for ourselves when we were boys?"

"Yes, now that I think about it." He turned to Athenor. "We went out there one spring day, but all we saw were the ruins. We didn't dare investigate them, though."

"But since then, surely you've learned more about them?" Athenor asked.

"Yes," Oreste replied. "That ruined house predates the f rst German and Dutch settlers here in 1700 – like the foundation in the middle of town. Perhaps they were both built by the same hands. Considering that the Lenape had European-style housing already, someone must have given them instruction. They could have built it, I suppose.

"Legend is that some early Dutchmen must have taught them. The Dutch were wide-ranging explorers during the last century – they built forts and settlements in what would become New York and parts of Pennsylvania."

"Yes," Athenor mused, "I know the Dutch formally declared New Netherland to be a province of the Dutch Republic in 1624. But this area is far away from their holdings. True, they had good trading relations with the Lenape, but why build such permanent structures here? Far from their population centers?"

"Who can say?" Oreste shrugged. "It's only one theory. It might have been built by some other group. But since the founding of Loreley, there have been stories about The White Lodge. That's what people have called it."

"Why?"

"Because of those travelers, of course," Ulysse rasped impatiently. "Supposedly, they thought it was an inn or tavern, and entered seeking shelter and hospitality."

"So, to them, it did not appear as ruins at all, but an intact house?" Athenor asked carefully, remembering its initial appearance before it faded into ruins.

"Just so," Oreste answered uneasily. "It would appear intact to them but once they entered, it would return to ruins – and they were never seen again."

"I had the same thought. But then, do you think it's the abode of the Winter Ghosts?"

"Yes. The ghosts and the house are connected somehow. They have mostly been seen in its vicinity…until lately. That congregant of Baldur's, I told you about – Gertrude Vogt."

"But you said you have no conjecture why they selected her in particular?"

"Neither does Baldur – at least so he's said to me." Oreste was reconsidering whether his friend had told him the entire truth.

"Is this it?" Ulysse interjected as they approached the Reformed Church parsonage. A few congregants were going in and out of the adjacent church for their morning prayers – led by an assistant pastor. Baldur was too ill at present to facilitate most services, only appearing at Sunday's Worship Service, as it was called in the Reformed Church.

The parsonage was smaller than Oreste's, reflecting the lesser congregation and its sponsorship. It was more a cottage than a house, with a single story, the usual architectural style, but with green ivy covering its walls, between which narrow windows peered. They went up to the door, and Ulysse sharply rapped. A feeble voice from inside bade them enter.

They opened the door and found themselves in a single room with a low ceiling and a fire in a hearth along one wall. A small kitchen was in one corner, with a hinged larder, pots, and pans hung on open cabinets, and a small countertop where food was prepared. Two armchairs with frayed and worn upholstery were placed close to the fire. Tufts of horsehair spurted here and there from the seat cushions.

A tiny circular table stood in the center of the room, with two stiff wooden chairs. On the other side of the room was an escritoire with its chair and a single bookcase crammed with bound and unbound books and folios perched precariously on its shelves. Several books and scrolls were piled atop the desk. There were candles set at various points around the room, adding to the firelight. For all of that, it was a dim and dismal sitting room.

It struck Athenor as a place where a hermit might live. There was no sign of feminine touches to suggest that Bella even lived there with her husband. As if she had no emotional investment in their home.

From a doorway on the far wall, the feeble voice called again. They went inside to find a small bedchamber, without pictures or windows. A double-sized featherbed dominated the room, with blankets and a drab bedspread.

Unexpectedly, Baldur was not in it. He lay on an adjacent, narrow daybed with a thin, green-colored mattress, propped against the headboard, with blankets pulled up to his chin. Candles set on two tabourets flanking the featherbed provided the only light. There was a small stool near the daybed.

Baldur appeared even more wan and frail than usual. Oreste noticed but assumed it was from the exertion of the day before. He smiled down at his friend and patted him on the shoulder.

"Why, you lazy lollpoop,[21] have you been abed all day?" He joked. Before Baldur could answer, he waved Athenor forward. "This is the physician I told you about – Dr. Athenor."

Baldur smiled faintly and struggled to lift a hand from beneath the blanket. Athenor held up his palm for pause.

---

[21] Meaning an idle or lazy man; so, Oreste's preface of "lazy" is an obvious redundancy.

"Pastor Rathenau," he said gently. "I'm pleased to make your acquaintance. And this," he nodded sidewise, "is Oreste's cousin, Ulysse."

"That's right," the former mayor said gruffly. "We'd like to ask you about the ghosts."

Athenor winced at Ulysse's customary lack of tact. "But first, Oreste has told me something of your ailment. Perhaps I can help you with that."

"I would be most grateful, Doctor." Baldur smiled faintly.

Athenor shed his cloak and hat and handed them to Oreste. Ulysse did likewise, not thinking of hanging them himself. Oreste grinned tolerantly and went back into the main room to hang them near the front door.

Athenor drew up the stool and sat. He rolled up the sleeves of his green deerskin overshirt and opened his medical satchel. Baldur propped himself on his elbows and noticed the long hip sheath for the scramasax knife.

"You don't use that to operate, I hope," he asked, half-joking.

Athenor smiled crookedly. "Only when a patient requires a lethal cure." He removed a listening trumpet from his bag. "Please unbutton your nightshirt. I want to examine your heartbeat."

Baldur reluctantly complied and as Athenor set one end of the trumpet to the shrunken chest and the other to his ear, he asked about symptoms.

"…No appetite, I'm constipated, pain…pain in my joints and stomach. And, just very, very tired, and weak."

Athenor replaced the trumpet in his satchel and palpated Baldur's abdomen and prodded at his muscles. Finally, on a suspicion, he had Baldur open his mouth and bare his teeth. Athenor gingerly lifted the lips and inspected the gumline.

His eyes narrowed. There was a bluish line where the gums met the teeth. He released the lips and leaned back on his stool and then rose to his feet. "Pastor Rathenau, I need to go into the next room and search for something. Will you excuse me?"

Baldur was clearly perplexed but waved his permission. Together with Oreste and Ulysse, Athenor proceeded back into the sitting room and summoned them into the kitchen. He examined the pots and pans hanging there and rubbed at their interiors.

"They're iron, aren't they?" Ulysse whispered. "Is the same thing as those foundry workers in Leichtenberg?"

"Similar. Those workers inhaled fumes filled with iron and lead particles. But iron cookware, popular as it seems to be in British America, only very rarely results in significant poisoning. No." He shook his head meditatively. "The bluish line on Baldur's gums is consistent with lead poisoning, not iron – as I've seen in potters and painters. And I recollect that in the Poitou region of France and also in Devon, there were outbreaks of colic in the last century from high levels of lead in their apple ciders."

"From the soils nourishing the apple trees?" Oreste asked.

"Possibly. Or possibly from the still-common practice of using lead presses to crush the apples."

"Hmph," Ulysse grunted. "Enough to make a man stick with beer or rum."

"But if Baldur has lead poisoning, where did he get it?" Oreste asked. "Not from the cookware. And unlikely to be from any other food or drink in this household. Or else Bella would have gotten it, too."

Athenor shrugged noncommittedly. But he realized that, unlike artisans who worked with lead pigments, Baldur's occupation would not bring him into frequent contact with lead. No, the route of poisoning was undoubtedly oral. And if he alone were affected and not the wife who lived with him, then…

But what to do about it? All he had was the diagnosis and his reasoning, not evidence of deliberate poisoning. He could scarcely count on Sheriff Richter's interest or support. But perhaps there was evidence lying somewhere around.

"Ulysse," he whispered, "I'd like for you to search this room, especially the kitchen. See if you can find a sack or a jar filled with gray or black powder."

"What…?" Ulysse began before Athenor cut him off.

"I'll explain later. In the meantime, Oreste and I will ask Baldur what he knows about the ghosts."

Ulysse threw up his hands with exasperation but started searching the cabinets. Athenor led Oreste into the bedchamber, where Baldur had sunk back down with fatigue.

Athenor resumed his stool while Oreste stood at his shoulder. "Baldur, I am still pondering your ailment and I promise you some relief soon. But in the meanwhile, perhaps you can help us with the ghosts."

"What do you want to know?"

"As much as you can tell us. I know you want to help rid Loreley of them as much as anyone."

Baldur was silent for a few minutes, evidently weighing how much to disclose. Finally, he let out a sigh and began:

"Most of what I know comes from Pastor Schraal. He is the one who knows more about the Winter Ghosts than anyone. He has studied old records, scrolls, and books for the past ten years, ever since the ghosts killed his wife…To begin, you probably know something of the White Lodge on Hop-Toad Road?"

"Yes," Athenor answered, "I have seen it – the ruins. And Oreste has told us something about it, how it predates the émigrés who founded Loreley. But not who built it."

"I can answer that," Baldur's voice sank to a hush. "When the Dutch came to America around the beginning of the 17th century, there was a missionary of the Moravian Brethren with them. You know, the denomination that was founded by Jan Huss in the 1400s in Moravia. This missionary's name was originally Mátyás Soványy. He supposedly was just an ordinary man, although one with an intense ambition – and it was not zeal to spread the Good News of salvation.

"He hungered for personal power and began to delve into corners of dark knowledge. That took him into nearby

Wallachia, in search of an ancient shrine that he believed would unlock unholy wisdom. Wallachia was then, as now, a suzerainty of the Ottoman Empire. His visit there was quite a daring undertaking, for he could easily have been killed for blasphemy by the Turks just for being a Christian.

"But he was not caught and did not stay long. However, when he returned to Moravia, he was a changed man – now gloomy and withdrawn. But his Order did not reject him – not at first. They took him with them, away from the menace that dwelt in Wallachia – or so they believed. They traveled to these shores and settled at Fort Nassau – the first Dutch trading post in what was later to become Albany.

"But his once-ordinary character continued to degenerate, accompanied by some unspecified physical changes. The Order expelled him, and he went off by himself into the wilderness. After that, the name of Mátyás Sovány was never spoken again. But rumors began to whisper of a sorcerer who called himself Lurkó Drögö – described as a shepherd with a crooked staff and a tall hat, who walked the forest trails in a long robe that always covered his feet.

"Eventually, he arrived in this vicinity, where only the Lenape dwelt. He found the ancient road, that the Lenape named Hop-Toad Road, and followed it to where it ended – the rubble of a foundation where some unguessable building once stood…"

"The foundation upon which Town Hall in Loreley was built?"

"Just so. Now, Pastor Schraal told me he heard of this from an elderly Lenape woman who was alive at the time.

She said that Drögö searched for something in the rubble but reportedly never found it. His evil powers intimidated and enslaved the local Lenape and he forced them to excavate the ruins, but they never found what he sought. All they found was a fossil of something, but this was nonetheless a discovery that gladdened the sorcerer's foul heart, and he always kept it close by.

"He continued to have them search, but also forced them to build him that white stone house to his design…"

"Do you think he also taught the Lenape how to build their houses and structures?" Athenor interrupted, remembering that when the German missionaries arrived at Cloud Village, it was already filled with European-style dwellings.

"Yes, they learned from him, and after he was gone, they used that knowledge for themselves. But, as I was saying, when Drögö moved into the lodge, he took that fossil with him. And then, things got even worse for the tribespeople…" Baldur paused to gaze somberly at the ceiling. "He began to demand human sacrifices."

Athenor frowned with disgust. "Do you know how the tribespeople were sacrificed?"

"Their flayed skins were used to wallpaper the inside of the White Lodge, where Drögö would sit on his throne, wrapped in his evil dreams," Baldur closed his eyes momentarily at the thought. "I assume they were still living when he unsheathed his knife."

"But he finally died or was killed? And his servants, the Winter Ghosts, now tenant the ruins?"

"Oh, no. You misunderstand," Baldur opened his eyes a fraction. "The Winter Ghosts were not his servants…They were his killers."

10. Der Seemansturm

Few visited the Seaman's Tower anymore, except for children from the Saint Boniface School on outings led by their schoolmaster. The adult townsfolk had long become inured to its charms – and not a few of them were made uneasy by what reposed inside.

It was one of the first structures built by the founders of Loreley Town in 1700, the brainchild of retired Royal Prussian Navy Captain Heinrich Kühleborn. It was 100 feet of sturdy, white-painted cedar with gray trim, the tallest building in town. It had three floors, capped by an observatory with multiple brass telescopes perched on pedestals at the four points of the compass. In the past, those had been purposed for stargazing, but now there was talk of posting a sentry or two to use them, in light of the war that had started to bloom last year with the French and their Indian allies.

They had always relied on their alliance with the local Lenape and the broader Iroquois Confederacy, especially those nearby Seneca who had a paternalistic relation with the Munsee branch of the Lenape. Loreley Town considered the only menace to be the Cayuga, the Oneida, and those other Senecas who dwelt south of Lake Ontar'io – all of which were allies of the French. Even though they dwelt hundreds of miles away, the Hurons also posed a potent threat. Their ferocious raiding parties ranged far.

Currently, the *Seemansturm* was more a museum than a watchtower, filled with artifacts from the town's early days, including many of the personal belongings of Captain

Kühleborn and fixtures taken from his sloop – ship's wheel, anchors, coils of rope, pieces of sail, brass fittings. And on the third floor was the sarcophagus enclosing his remains, set squarely in the middle of the polished black oak flooring. The carven lid was adorned with nautical motifs and figures, including depictions of mermaids, octopi, and sea serpents, and delicately carved replicas of cresting waves and whirlpools. At its foot was a metal donation box perched on a small pedestal with a placard proclaiming advanced gratitude for any contribution to help defray maintenance costs – a rather tawdry appeal well in keeping with the character of the long-dead captain.

Children, expectedly, were fascinated by the sarcophagus, adults less so, for it was said that Kühleborn was one of the first émigrés to fall victim to the Winter Ghosts. Yet, even before his death, his contemporaries had eagerly hoped for it. It seems that to fund the tower's construction, he had accumulated subscriptions, announcing that it would be a maritime museum open to the public.

Yet, when it was finished, he made it his residence and forbade entry to all. Enraged, the subscribers brought suit against him, petitioning the court in Philadelphia to send a magistrate judge to oversee it. That, in turn, led to the creation of the Pastorius County Courthouse and a local judiciary.

In due time, the subscribers won their suit and got some of their monies returned – but pointedly had no interest in visiting the place afterward. Embittered, Kühleborn became a recluse and went so far as to build a balcony off the second story with a small wooden closet. Inside the closet was a commode with an open bottom, from which his bodily filth dropped onto the ground below.

It was while inside his closet that Kühleborn met his end, and his desiccated remains were eventually discovered by his charwoman. Despite the call of some folk that his body be dumped into one of the local cesspits, cooler heads prevailed and acceded to his written last wishes and entombed him in his own tower. Since then, it had genuinely become the maritime museum he had once promised.

Some of these thoughts passed through Judge Maximilian Lindt's mind as he leaned over the railing of the observatory. Puttering around at the other side was his bailiff, Timon Bierhals, fidgeting as he always did. Lindt also tried to curb his impatience.

Why on earth did Dr. Kitzler want to meet here of all places? What was the problem with meeting at his home, which sat at the foot of the tower? As he thought that, a smirk tugged at his lips, for he knew that the physician's house was built on the site below the long unused commode. *What was that Scripture verse Pastor von Mardure quoted in his sermon the other Sunday? Something about how only a fool builds his house upon sand? And what would the Bible say about a house built upon shite?*

But he had to admit that Kitzler had provided him with some medical relief for his gout. Bloodletting had eased some of his pain and stiffness. Otherwise, he would never have been able to climb up to the observatory, even with Bierhals' help. *But if he drains any more blood, I won't have enough left to invigorate a sparrow.*

He gazed out at the town below, drowsing in the afternoon sunlight. Loreley Town was crowded with trees, especially along the lazy, winding Paradise River that flowed through it. Many of the rooftops were painted green as well so that it almost looked like one great sea that the wind rippled. To the south, he could see the outlines of emerald and umber vegetable fields confined within their zigzagging wooden fences. In the distance, he could make out neat farmhouses and barns tossed here and there like a handful of white and red pebbles.

His reverie was interrupted by the sound of ascending feet from the circular stairwell. He snatched up his cane from where it was propped against the rail and hobbled inside, leaving the door to the observation deck open behind him. Gradually, a silver-trimmed black tricorn rose into view, followed by Athaulf Kitzler's smug face.

"Luckily for us," he said smoothly, "it's Friday and the courthouse is closed."

"In that case, why didn't we have this meeting in my chambers there?" Lindt snapped.

"Too many prying eyes nearby." Kitzler climbed onto the polished black oak floor and knuckled his back. In truth, he had hoped that climbing the tower would have exhausted the judge enough to wear down any resistance to his sales talk. "Speaking of which…" He nodded toward Bierhals, who was ambling inside from the deck.

"He can be trusted. But your missive…" Lindt withdrew a folded sheet of paper from the pocket of his coat, "promised a guaranteed cure for my gout at last?"

Kitzler came close to the judge, chewing at his blond mustache. "Yes, it is guaranteed to restore health, if you pray daily while holding it against the afflicted parts of your body."

"Oh? Guaranteed by whom?" Lindt eyed him suspiciously. "For the £500 you quoted?"

"I will guarantee it," Kitzler replied confidently. "Like anything else, you must give it time. But if it fails, I will refund your money." *Unless you happen to die first*, he thought hopefully.

"If it fails," Lindt said ominously, "I'll have you sent on a charge of fraud to High Street Prison in Philadelphia."[22]

"Now, now, Your Honor." He attempted a sycophantic smile. "I can only promise something to the extent of my knowledge. Admittedly, religious remedies are chancy by nature. But I suppose everything truly depends on how much you want to be healed." His voice turned eagerly oleaginous.

But he was beginning to have doubts about the wisdom of transacting with someone as powerful as Lindt. Perhaps he would be better off selling it to Schraal after all, who desperately wanted it. He would not get as much money as from Lindt, but there could be no question of Schraal's refusal. He congratulated himself on his forethought for sending Alistair Nathan to Cloud Village with an exploratory offer a couple of hours ago.

"I want to be healed," Lindt's eyes were icy, "but not by any mirage that depends solely upon my hopes. What kind

---

[22] A stone prison and workhouse were erected in 1720 in Philadelphia at the corner of Third and High Streets.

of idiot do you take me for?" He shook his head angrily. "You've done nothing but waste my time today – and made me climb these miserable steps to this miserable tower of shite. Trying to gull me, were you? I bid you Good Day, sir!"

He waved Bierhals to him irritably. The bailiff, who had listened to everything with bland indifference, stirred himself to his side and lent a hand to the judge's elbow. As they slowly descended the staircase, Kitzler heard Lindt's dwindling grumble, "Trying to gull me!"

Kitzler had to catch his breath and stifle his anger. *The nerve of the man! How dare he threaten me? Maybe he'll take a tumble down those stairs and break his stringy neck!*

He reached into the pocket of his coat and fingered the velvet sack inside. He wandered back to the rail and peered down at the entranceway far below. He was almost tempted to spit as the top of Lindt's head emerged alongside that of Bierhals.

But he felt a motion in the air behind him and turned to look back into the observatory. Even materialistic and unspiritual as he was, his animal instincts sensed a presence in the unlighted chamber, while motes danced in the wan sunbeams slanting onto the floor. He dimly felt an awareness of something standing still in the shadows just outside the pools of light.

Something that was equally aware of him and scrutinizing him.

His lips parted soundlessly, and he felt frozen in place, and a weary lassitude swept over him as if his strength were being slowly siphoned away. The air in that dark recess swirled faintly and within it were twin dark-blue pinpoints that might have been eyes in an oscillating shadowy nimbus. Below them was a dim glimmering crescent of needle-like teeth. And now, a soft, wordless whisper came from within the folds of whirling winds, and spidery, black fingers began to slowly reach out for him.

With effort, he snapped free from his immobility and looked down at the velvet bag in his hand, realizing it was what the ghost sought. Thinking quickly, he spun and dropped the sack over the rail.

Even as he did, he felt a rush of air streak past him, following the sack down. He felt momentarily giddy, and the tricorn was blown from his head to flutter over the side. He gripped the rail with both hands and leaned out to look down.

He saw the shadowy vortex plummeting toward the figures of Lindt and Bierhals, who stood still in conversation in front of the entrance. He saw the velvet sack drop unnoticed behind them. Then, they noticed the disturbance in the air and looked up in time to see what appeared to be an animate cloud just before it enveloped them.

A frightened wail drifted up as they staggered apart from each other. Lindt began fiercely swatting with his cane at the rotating wind while Bierhals dropped to all fours — atop the sack lying nearby. Kitzler saw the whirlwind divert from Lindt to fasten upon his bailiff.

Momentarily freed from the swathing vortex, Lindt stumbled away, redoubling his screams. If they had not noticed before, passersby now started running to his aid, and their cries began to swell. Bierhals' own cries died to a prolonged moan, and within the folds of the rotating wind, his body collapsed and began to shrivel. Then, the ghost turned to Lindt, and his garments began to whip with its wind. The cane fell from Lindt's hand and his scream changed to a groan.

By that time the townsfolk had drawn near, some with upraised canes. The shadowy vortex withdrew from Lindt and hesitated as if deliberating whether to confront them. Then, with what seemed to be a frustrated wail, it swirled away from Lindt and raced off into the trees.

Kitzler saw a path form among the green, tossing treetops, burrowing between them in the direction of the Paradise River flowing through the southwestern part of town. He squinted after the runnel for long minutes and noticed other similar paths form and converge upon it until they were all lost in the swishing ocean of trees.

His attention was then redirected to the gathering crowd below. Some were bending over Bierhals' body solicitously. Nearby, Lindt was feebly trying to rise but then abruptly collapsed into the arms of several townsmen.

Kitzler thought quickly. It might be incriminating if the judge were to relay details of their rendezvous and conversation. *But maybe, under my tender care, he never would.*

"Take him to my clinic! Quickly, now! His life is at stake!" he yelled down. Several townsmen waved their acknowledgment and gingerly lifted Lindt and carried him in the direction of the *Mediclin Klinik*. "I'll be down in a minute!"

But he was less concerned with Lindt than with the velvet bag that lay beneath Bierhals' corpse.

"Don't touch the bailiff!" he added. "It might be dangerous!"

A few townsfolk who had been cautiously hovering above Bierhals quickly stepped back. Kitzler darted from the railing and began dashing down the staircase to retrieve the bag before it was discovered.

After all, it was still worth some profit if he could sell it to Schraal.

But he now realized that what Baldur told Bella was true – that the ghosts wanted the gem badly enough to kill for it. Clearly, it was too dangerous to hide on his person or even in his lodgings.

As he hurried down past the third floor, he paused, and his gaze fell on the Kühleborn's sarcophagus and the donation box at its feet. And a smile curved his lips.

11. The Dungeon of the Angels

Athenor was still contemplating Baldur's last words when Ulysse returned from the kitchen with a grim expression, holding a small cloth sack tied with a string. He waited at the entrance to the bedchamber and Athenor excused himself to Baldur to join him. He carefully untied the string from the offered bag and peered inside. He dipped a finger and then patted his tongue with it. He scowled and gestured to Ulysse, who re-tied the sack.

By that time, Oreste's curiosity had impelled him near and Athenor whispered some words to him. The pastor's face fell with a mixture of surprise, anger, and sorrow. He gave one last pitying glance to Baldur who still lay on the daybed, then exited the room. There came the sound of the front door opening and closing in the sitting room.

Athenor returned to Baldur, who had been oblivious to what had just transpired. The physician sat on the stool and gently patted the pastor's hand. As Baldur blinked back awake, Athenor continued softly,

"Excuse me, Pastor Rathenau…Baldur. Pray, continue. You were saying the Winter Ghosts killed the sorcerer Drögö…"

"Yes. Yes, that is what Nikolasz said he learned from the elderly Lenape woman at Cloud Village. As I said, Drögö had become a terror to them, and they finally resolved to kill him. So, their medicine man made offerings and prayers to their creator-god *Ketanëtuwit* — but to no avail. He then turned to the dark gods and spirits. He dared not pray to the prime god of evil, *Mahtantu*, because he feared that terrible deity was already in league with the sorcerer. Nor would he think about summoning the evil serpent, *Maxáxâk*, or the cannibal ice-giant *Mhuwe*…"

"I know that one," Athenor murmured. That was the Lenape name for the *Giwakwa* of Abenaki legend – a being he had encountered in 1742 when it destroyed Fort White Pine and indirectly killed his wife, Chenoa.

"…but there were other dark spirits that sometimes could be merciful to men," Baldur was saying.

"The Thunder-Beings?" Athenor's thoughts returned to the legends of the *Pèthakhue*.

"You know them?" Baldur whispered. "The spirits who live in the sky and cause lightning and storms? Who sometimes kill people but sometimes will also rescue them if that is their whim?"

"So, the Winter Ghosts are the Thunder-Beings summoned to defeat Drögö?"

"In part. They are called the Children of the Storm, the Children of *Pèthakhue*. They are miniature versions of a Thunder-Being."

"The tornado!" exclaimed Ulysse, who had come up alongside the physician.

"Just so," sighed Baldur. "*Pèthakhue* answered the medicine man's prayers and brought his children to kill Drögö. And they did. They entered his white mansion in the woods and drained the life from him. I suppose his shriveled corpse yet remains there to this day."

"But they did not leave after that," Athenor said.

"No. They found that they enjoyed killing humans and took the White Lodge for their own home, and it became a ghost itself — materializing at times to lure unsuspecting travelers inside."

"But their father, the tornado being, did not approve of their depredations? And has tried to seize them back into the clouds when he can?"

"Where did you hear that?" This was clearly news to Baldur.

"We've seen it happen," Ulysse interjected.

"And we understand why the ghosts have appeared mainly during the winter months — when tornados are rare and weak," Athenor added.

"I never suspected that. Neither does Nikolasz. We both thought the tornado and its children were all of the same accord." Baldur tapered off into rumination.

"Do you know, Pastor, why the ghosts have become emboldened lately?" Athenor pursued, "If my conjecture is correct — that the tornado-spirit *Pèthakhue* truly is trying to curb his rebellious children — why would the ghosts strike during the spring? When tornadoes are at their peak of power? To strike even here in town?"

Baldur did not answer for long minutes, then gave a resigned exhalation and inclined his head a fraction. "They seek a talisman – one they know can destroy them." He lifted a bony finger to point toward the doorway. "On my desk, there are some drawings…"

Athenor nodded to Ulysse, who left the room, then listened patiently as Baldur continued,

"I learned all of this from Nikolasz, and I copied a woodcut of the talisman that he showed me. He said he found it in an old, iron-bound book from the Middle Ages that he kept from when he was a student in Heidelberg. Where he found that book, he never said…"

He was interrupted by Ulysse's return, bearing the sack in one hand and several pieces of parchment. He handed the latter to Athenor, who sifted through them. He held up one that appeared to be a page torn from a book with a color painting. It depicted an angelic being garbed in a black robe in the act of ravishing a woman whose clothes were in disarray. Beneath the painting was printed:

Genesis 6:2: "The sons of God saw the daughters of men that they were fair, and they took them wives of all which they chose."

Athenor realized this was a depiction of one of the evil angels from the early days of mankind that mated with human females and fathered human or human-like children, the *Nephilim*. In those times, it was said, such angels were not spirits but made of unholy flesh and blood.

The next paper had a pencil reproduction of a woodcut that depicted a stone wall with a gateway. The gateway was an oval, above which were two circular openings – meant to resemble a gigantic face. Underneath it was the Latin transcription,

CARCEREM ANGELORUM

QUA VIA FINES

"Do you recognize that, Seth?" Ulysse hovered over his shoulder.

"Yes. I've seen it before in ancient books. It says, 'The Dungeon of the Angels' and 'Where the Road Ends.' The legend is that the evil fathers of the *Nephilim* were punished by God with imprisonment in an underground dungeon far from any human habitation. The last bit about the road ending is believed to be a sardonic metaphor for their fate. There are a host of tales about its ancient location – Ottoman Anatolia, China, the Karakorum Desert, the Viceroyalty of New Spain in the Lower Americas, even in Dai Nippon Teikoku."[23]

"I remember something about that, come to think of it. Also, something about a guardian placed at the entrance?"

Athenor nodded. "A three-headed creature. Greek mythology calls it Cerberus. Other legends say it was a different kind of creature, a female creature named *Velnias*. She appears in various mythologies. For instance, Russian legends refer to *Vlasezhelische* or 'The Entrance to the Underground Kingdom Where *Velnias* Dwells.' However, I've not seen any pictorial representation of her."

---

[23] What Japan was called in those times; it had already been visited in the 1500s by Portuguese traders and in the 1600s by Jesuit missionaries. A highly educated man like Athenor would have heard of it.

He flipped to the final page and found another sketch, this one of a gem set in a rectangle of plain metal. There were Latin words inscribed underneath:

OCULIS VELNIAS

CUSTODIS MALORUM ANGELORUM

"The Eye of Velnias and the Warden of the Evil Angels," Athenor translated quietly. He returned to the depiction of the gateway and found a tiny rectangle positioned above the gaping "mouth." He tapped that with his finger. "The 'eye' was said to be a talisman owned by *Velnias*, endowing her with power."

"That kind of power is impressive, isn't it?" Baldur said. "That made *Velnias* one of the mightiest of creatures, although one forever chained to the gateway, unable to use that power elsewhere. But at some time in the ancient past, she was somehow slain, and the gem was stolen to vanish into myth and legend. And with her disappearance, the gateway was shut and those evil angels inside were imprisoned forever. Nikolasz thinks it was the object Drögö was searching for in the ruined foundation but never found."

"You say the gem is a talisman of power?" Ulysse asked. "What kind of power could it give to someone who found it?"

"Nikolasz told me he believed it could restore life to the dead. And maybe could even restore the health of a living person." Baldur's voice became wistful for a moment.

"And you say the ghosts are afraid of this gem and seek to prevent it from falling into other hands?" Athenor asked. "Do you know why they fear it?"

"I don't know. If Nikolasz knows, he has not shared the answer with me. He says he wants to use it to resurrect his dead wife Rosamund – who was killed by the ghosts. But I've begun to think he's lying about that. I think his hatred for the ghosts is stronger than the love for his long-dead wife."

"I don't believe the ghosts would be worried about any resurrection of Rosamund. They are afraid it would empower someone to defeat them." Athenor's eyes narrowed in thought.

"Drögö, do you think?" Ulysse interjected. "To raise his spirit from the dead? From his corpse that still lies inside the White Lodge?"

Athenor considered this for several minutes, then shook his head. "Possibly. The ghosts defeated him before – but that was when he did not possess the gem."

"If that is Nikolasz's intention, he has not told me," Baldur said gravely. "I've begun to wonder if he intends to use the gem on himself – to gain enough power to kill the ghosts. And the Thunder- Being, too. To destroy them all. He told me that to use the gem, one must know the proper incantations. But when I've pressed him to tell me more about that, he becomes vague and evasive."

Athenor digested all of that. "I think we can agree – based upon what we know – that the gem *must* in some way have the power to destroy the ghosts, or else they would not fear it. Or seek it. And since they seek it here in town, it must have resurfaced here."

"Why here of all places?" Ulysse asked. "How did it get here from China or any of the other supposed locations?"

"Nikolasz told me he believes when it was stolen, the thief fled across the world and carried it here ages ago, where he died or lost it," Baldur replied.

"Do you know if it's been rediscovered in the foundation recently?" Athenor asked.

Baldur shook his head. "Not so far as I know. Nikolasz would come into town and search for it there until the tenants became suspicious of him. He asked me to search for him, but I've been too weak. I, in turn, asked one of my congregants to search, especially since she was a common sight there. Gertrude Vogt."

"The charwoman? Did she find it?"

Baldur expelled his breath slowly. "If she did, she never told me. Then, Town Hall burned down."

"Not by the charwoman, though?"

Baldur hesitated before answering. "No. I think it was Nikolasz, but I have no proof. He was becoming more and more frustrated and believed it was secreted somewhere in the foundation. I think he wanted to erase Town Hall to make it easier to search – fewer prying eyes. Since then, he has been seen sniffing around the rubble on several occasions. I doubt he has found it yet."

"But *someone* must have found it, or the ghosts would not be prowling and killing in town."

"Yes, I suppose that's correct," Baldur replied. "But found by whom? Bella and I searched Gertrude's room. We did not find it there. Bella looked everywhere…"

"And you trust your wife's word?" Athenor's expression became sad.

As Baldur struggled to understand, the front door opened, and they heard footsteps and the rumble of voices. Athenor rose to his feet to see Oreste leading a scowling Sheriff Richter into the bedchamber.

"Doctor," Richter's voice hovered between irritation and alarm. "Is it true? What Pastor Von Mardure told me?"

Ulysse extended the cloth sack and opened it. "Taste it yourself."

Richter dipped a finger into the gray powder inside and dabbed some on his tongue. He grimaced. "I've molded enough musket-balls to recognize lead." He wiped his hand on his trousers and turned to Athenor. "And you say Baldur here has the symptoms of lead poisoning?"

"I invite you to examine his gum line, with the unmistakable sign of chronic lead deposition." Athenor gestured toward Baldur whose face showed bafflement and an emerging realization. "I think you will also find that his wife Bella has no similar sign or symptoms."

Richter was rubbing the hair on his ears contemplatively when more footsteps sounded in the sitting room and they all turned to see Bella enter, shrugging the shawl from her shoulders. She darted a worried glance at them all and then locked eyes with Baldur. There was a look of ineffable sadness on his face.

"So, Johanna was right about you." Oreste glared at Bella. He remembered Baldur tottering on the stairs at Gertrude's rooming house and Bella's seeming carelessness — and now realized it was not carelessness at all.

At his side, Richter said nothing but bent her a frowning stare. Ulysse wordlessly lifted the sack and dangled it mockingly before her.

Athenor smiled thinly but his eyes were hard. "Why, *Frau* Rathenau, what curious seasonings you have in your cupboard."

12. Nikolasz Schraal

The sun was sliding down toward the distant *Achpateuny Kihatënink* – the West Wind Mountains. The tall pines on the slopes of their eastern counterpart threw lengthening shadows across the palisade of Cloud Village. The few villagers still around were straggling to their houses. A group of boys was defying the dimming light by continuing their game of *pahsaheman*, a Lenape version of soccer. Sitting to one side was Hans Martens, watching the youths enviously, for he had never been invited to play with them.

His brother Gabriël was standing on the porch between the twin doorways of the East Wind Reformed Church, shaking hands with villagers departing the evening prayer service. A wind had risen from the mountains behind, gently tugging at the kerchiefs of the women.

Inside the small parsonage at the rear of the church, Nikolasz Schraal lit the last of the candles in his study and reseated himself at his desk. It was piled high with various books, some of which were bound in iron with rusty clasps, others were scrolls and folios. The walls were lined with bookcases, their shelves overflowing with still more books and documents. No cross was fixed to any wall, but on the one behind the desk, a curious animal skull was secured by pegs. It was the size of a human cranium but with eyes on the sides of the narrow head and a long beak filled with back-curving saw-like teeth. Fastened to the wall beneath it was a curved ivory-handed *khukuri* knife with a 10-inch blade of polished steel.

He was penciling notes on a paper before him, rechecking his conclusions.

Kaxkxàkës Métëme: "Hop-Toad Road — for most of the 1600s, under nominal Dutch control. But only the Lenape were dwelling in the northeastern part of what would become Pennsylvania Province. The road that ended in the middle of Loreley. Drögö knew where he was going. Of all the roads in this world, this must be the one."

Schraal circled the last entry, relinquished his pencil, and leaned back in his chair contemplatively.

Foolish to keep re-evaluating, he told himself. *This must be where the gem was lost — and where it will be found. It's only a matter of time before the Oculus Velnias falls into my hands.*

Those same hands knotted with anger. He jumped up from his chair and started pacing the narrow space between the desk and the windows. Outside, he could hear the happy cries and shouts of the boys playing soccer, but all that did was irritate him further.

Just then, he flinched back as a face popped up right outside the window. He clenched his teeth with surprise and then resentment.

"Hans Martens!" he shouted. "What the devil do you think you're about?"

Hans merely grinned widely and planted his face against the glass, mischievously repeating "No, no, no," in his sing-song voice.

"Damn you! Can't you say anything else?"

Unfazed, Hans kissed the glass as if to show forgiveness for the pastor's outburst, then stopped smiling and shook his head sadly. "Don't, don't don't..." He abruptly turned at a cry from his brother and wandered off, leaving Schraal speechless.

He wondered if that had not been Hans' usual nonsensical palilalia but a genuine communication. From Cholena perhaps? A warning?

He shook away the thought. Ever since Rosamund's murder, he had set his mind. Nothing was going to deter him from his vengeance. The Winter Ghosts must be destroyed, even if it cost him his life – or the life of anyone else.

He wondered if Baldur Rathenau had already found the gem but decided to keep it for himself. He had let that fool think it might cure him of his illness with "incantations" – a useful lie to secure his help. The gem had only one use, gave power to only one kind of...Being.

He had also let him believe that he wanted the gem to resurrect Rosamund. But he had long realized that would be futile. Her spirit had departed to Heaven at the death of her body and would not return to it. All that he could resurrect would be a body without a soul – a pathetic creature at best and a murderous monster at worst.

Oh Baldur, you dolt. If you only realized any of this – or realized who the evil spirit truly was who possessed Mátyás Sovány in that shrine in Wallachia...

His thoughts were interrupted by a timid rap at the door. It eased open to show an abashed Gabriël Martens.

"I crave your pardon, Pastor," he said cautiously. "I'm sorry that Hans has been annoying you. He's unusually agitated today."

Schraal swatted away the apology with a grunt, then hesitated. "Has he been listening to your elderly lodger?"

"Why, yes. How did you know? They spent some time together and afterward, Hans bolted out of the house and has been wandering around the village for hours. I finally caught sight of him at your window as I was ending the evening prayer service."

"It's nothing." But Schraal wondered what Cholena had conveyed to her clairaudient puppet. "Is there anything else?" He returned to his chair and leaned his elbows on the desk.

"Yes, Pastor. You have a visitor, Alistair Nathan from the Kitzler Clinic in Loreley." Gabriël edged aside to let the nurse pass into the room.

The nurse's clothes were wrinkled, spattered with the dust of travel. He scowled around the room as if expecting bats to flutter from the top of the bookcases.

"You're Nikolasz Schraal?" he asked petulantly. When the Pastor inclined his head, Nathan reached inside his coat pocket and withdrew a sealed letter, and tossed it onto the table. "I hope you realize how long a trip it was from town."

Schraal eyed him narrowly and used a penknife to cut the red wax seal and unfold the letter. He read a bit, then asked, "You are a nurse to Dr. Kitzler, then?" When Nathan nodded, he continued, "Did he tell you what was in this letter?"

"If he wanted me to know, he wouldn't have waxed it shut," Nathan replied tersely. "He only told me to ask if his terms were 'acceptable.' If so, he wants you to come to town to the clinic to seal the bargain."

Schraal inspected the rest of the missive and gave a mirthless smile. "You may convey that his terms are 'acceptable.' Did the doctor say when he wanted me to come to town?"

"The sooner the better. He said if you wanted to ride back with me, that would be all right." The tone of Nathan's voice suggested he hoped the offer would be declined.

"I need some time to prepare. You may tell Kitzler I will arrive at his clinic sometime tomorrow. And now, if there is nothing else, you have stayed your welcome," he said with finality. *Several minutes of this dunderhead's company was more than enough, let alone a ride of some hours to Loreley!*

Gabriël looked embarrassed. "Uh, night is coming on. Perhaps we could offer Mr. Nathan lodging until tomorrow?"

"Thank you, no." The nurse almost recoiled with distaste. "I will be heading back now, night or not."

"As you wish," Schraal waved a dismissive hand. Needing no further urging, Nathan pivoted and strode briskly from the room. Gabriël shrugged apologetically and withdrew, closing the door.

After a few minutes, Schraal rose again and began to pace, half-elated, half apprehensive. He went to the animal skull fixed to the wall and ran a caressing finger along its long snout.

"Soon," he whispered. "Soon, my beauty. For I think I know where your sister is, and I will return to her what she lost…And then you will tremble, *Wintergeister*. Oh, yes, you will."

He paused as Hans' voice echoed from outside, a dwindling refrain of "Don't, don't, don't…" that died away into the twilight.

13. Kitzler Medical Clinic

By the time Sheriff Richter fastened the manacles onto Bella, four congregants from Saint Boniface arrived at Baldur's parsonage. Oreste had left word before leaving the Sheriff's Office with a passerby from his church.

Bella glared sullenly at Athenor while her wrists were shackled, correctly identifying him as the one who had discovered her murder scheme. But she said nothing, not even to Baldur, who remained in the bedchamber and whose eyes were bright with tears. She did not even bother to look at him.

"I'll be taking her to our gaol now." Richter began leading her out, as the congregants made way for them.

"One word, Sheriff," Athenor said. "Don't tell anyone about the method Bella used just yet. We might be able to use that to our advantage later."

"That's wise," Richter replied grudgingly. "But I'll continue to question Bella."

"And see if she has any accomplices," Ulysse rasped, offering Richter the sack of powdered lead.

"If she does, someone will talk — especially her fellow worshippers at the Reformed Church," Oreste added. "Gossipers are always the plague of any congregation. Someone there will have seen or heard something." Oreste waved the congregants toward the bedchamber with instructions to carry Baldur out.

Athenor rose from the escritoire where he had been penning a note. He replaced the quill pen into its stand and waved the paper to dry the ink.

"Oreste." He motioned the pastor over and handed it to him. "Have Johanna feed Baldur a diet rich in these foodstuffs. No alcohol, plenty of water."

Oreste read the list aloud, "Lemons, apples, garlic, wild blueberries. Seems a very simple remedy. Does it truly work?"

"I've had luck in the past using these to bleed out at least some of the deposits of lead or iron from the body. Nothing, I fear, will restore his health completely, but these along with the stoppage of his poisoning will hopefully stabilize him. He will have a long recovery – to whatever level of health he can achieve."

"Is this a common remedy? Something that Dr. Kitzler might use?"

"I've learned many remedies from the Native peoples, who often seem more astute with their treatments. But I'm afraid most Provincial physicians would be prescribing purgatives and brandy. A wrongheaded cure since those both deplete the body of its water and weaken it."

The four men came out of the bedchamber, carrying Baldur in an improvised stretcher made up from blankets. They paused as Oreste drew close and laid a hand on Baldur's arm.

"You'll be all right, my friend." He smiled down into Baldur's still sorrowful eyes. "I'm having you taken to my home. Johanna will look after you. Dr. Athenor will be your physician now."

"Not Kitzler?" Relief flooded Baldur's face.

"Hardly. He's had his chance at doctoring you." Oreste locked eyes with the four men and gave them a nod. "Gently now, it's a fair distance to my house."

One of them shook his head. "I've brought a wagon, Pastor. When you told us in front of Richter's office what was about, I reckoned *Herr* Rathenau would need one."

Oreste clapped him on the shoulder and motioned them toward the front door. "I'm going with him, of course." He took down his cloak and hat from beside the door. "I'll see you later at my home," he told Athenor and Ulysse and followed the rest outside.

No sooner had the creak and clatter of the horse-drawn wagon faded down the lane than they heard a quick drum of bootheels at the door. From the deepening twilight, a figure in a blue uniform appeared and they saw it was Deputy Georg Herbst, nervously chewing his mustache.

Athenor was puzzled. The deputy had not accompanied Richter. The last he had seen of him was at the Sheriff's Office when they first arrived in town.

"Richter just left," Ulysse volunteered, "if that's who you're seeking."

"I'm not here…for him," Herbst panted, removing his shako to sleeve his brow. "It's you I wanted to find, Doctor."

Athenor moved closer to him and waited until the deputy caught his breath.

"My pardon," Herbst wheezed. "I've run all the three miles from the *Seemansturm*. I…I do need to see the sheriff, but I thought of you first, Doctor. I overheard what you said about the ghosts back at the office…"

"Tell me."

Between gasps, the deputy related what had happened at the tower a little while before — and the townsfolk who witnessed the attack on Bierhals and Lindt.

"…so, they *are* real. I was too late there to see for myself, but honest men and women saw it. And saw Bierhals alive one minute and white and shrunken the next…"

"Your sheriff probably still won't believe it," Ulysse added dryly.

"That's why I came here first." Herbst spoke to Athenor. "I thought you'd be the one to know what to do."

A bit too late to do Bierhals any good. Athenor thought, but only replied, "And Lindt — is he still alive?"

"Barely. They just finished carrying him to the Kitzler clinic. Dr. Kitzler is with him now."

Athenor's eyes narrowed in thought. He turned to Ulysse. "Are you ready to pay a visit to the clinic?"

"I've been ready for the past five minutes," Ulysse grunted, taking his cloak down from near the door and handing Athenor his. They quickly threw them on and retrieved their slouch hats.

As Herbst led the way outside, Athenor paused at the threshold and looked back into the sitting room.   *Yes,* he thought somberly. *Almost no trace that a woman ever lived here, that she had the slightest investment in her house…or her husband.*

He gently closed the front door, wondering if Baldur would ever return here – or to his church, for that matter. He assumed that the same Assistant Pastors who currently substituted for him would continue. Even if he lived, Baldur would be an invalid. Surely, he had deserved better.

He followed Herbst and Ulysse down the lane as a lamplighter teetered on his ladder and set his smoldering linstock to a whale-oil lantern set in a glass box atop a high pole. The Kitzler Medical Clinic was not far. They saw a small group of townsfolk just starting to file out its door. Their faces were marked by a mixture of sadness, anger, and…fear.

Herbst laid a hand on a grizzled merchant's elbow. "What's happened, Hartung?"

The merchant nervously scratched his long side whiskers. "He's dead. We were just told. So, now they're both dead – Bierhals and Lindt. We were just told."

"But he was alive not fifteen minutes ago," Herbst exclaimed.

Hartung shrugged and repeated stolidly, "We were just told." He squirmed away from Herbt's hand and joined the others in trudging down the lane, following the string of yellow lamps.

Athenor pushed forward, dodging the last folk, and caught the door before it closed. The dark-haired male nurse gave a start and stepped back into the waiting room.

"I'm sorry, but the doctor is not receiving anyone just now." The man said anxiously.

"And you are?" Athenor asked coolly.

"Humphrey Kellett. Nurse Kellett." He thrust out his chin, trying to appear firm.

But the physician hardly glanced at him, searching the sitting room, and spotting the hallway leading to the examination rooms.

"Where is Judge Lindt?" he rapped out.

"Second door on the right," Kellett managed to squeak out.

Athenor pushed past him, followed by Ulysse, who took off his hat and smirked at the discomfited nurse. Herbst trailed after them, puffing to keep up.

They all made their way to the designated door and Athenor nearly bumped into Kitzler exiting it.

"I beg your pardon," Kitzler said irritably. "You are not permitted inside my patient rooms."

Herbst came up and tilted his chin truculently. "I've asked Dr. Athenor to see Judge Lindt."

Kitzler reddened with anger but controlled himself. "Well, *Mister* Athenor, you've come too late. I'm afraid the judge is beyond the help of any quaint Native nostrums of yours."

Athenor leaned forward until their faces were only a few inches apart. "In that case," he said coldly, "you won't mind if I examine his body."

"Why?" Kitzler blinked, unable to meet that steely glare.

"I've already told Dr. Athenor about the attack by the ghosts," Herbst interjected. "Now that they're established as genuine, I want him to inspect the bodies – Lindt and Bierhals."

Kitzler fidgeted, pursing his lips. "Fine. Bierhals is in the next room."

"I'll see Lindt first if you don't mind." Athenor wondered if Kitzler was trying to stall – and if so, why?

Kitzler grudgingly stepped aside and Athenor entered the room, followed by Ulysse and Herbst. The latter shut the door in Kitzler's face.

Lindt's body lay on a low bed in the yellow light thrown from a candle chandelier. The room was not large, with dark cedar walls filled with glass-doored cabinets. Several low tabourets held surgical instruments neatly arranged upon white cloths.

Athenor handed his hat to Ulysse and threw back his cloak. He bent to the bed and gingerly removed the blanket from the corpse.

Maximilian Lindt lay face up, still in his waistcoat and trousers that were littered with dirt and leaf debris. His crumpled coat lay on the floor. The collar of his cotton shirt had been loosened. His head had been thrown back, his lips were parted, his eyes closed.

Athenor laid a hand on the wrinkled forehead. It was still warm to the touch. He bent his head to scrutinize the face, noticing several scratches – one on the left upper eyelid, a second below the right eye. There were some slight bruises on the lower lip. He then gently prised open the eyelids and saw small speckles of blood in the whites. He closed the lids again and lifted the head, bending to inspect the back, finding the hair all awry, loosened from its ribbon. He laid the head down and straightened.

"He doesn't look like Kikkert's body at all," Ulysse murmured. "Instead of being pallid, his face looks a bit reddish."

"No, not like Kikkert at all," Athenor replied noncommittally.

"If he wasn't killed by the ghost, what did it?" Herbst asked. "Are those scratches anything?"

"I'm not certain. You say witnesses report that he was tossed about by the ghost – which would explain the debris on his clothing. Perhaps similar debris caused the scratches. It could be a case of a weak heart coupled with shock. I'm sure that's what Dr. Kitzler's diagnosis would be."

Ulysse eyed him dubiously, guessing his friend was not telling all he suspected. "Deputy Herbst, can you kindly go outside and tell Kitzler we will be seeing Bierhals presently?"

The deputy's forehead wrinkled with puzzlement, but he nodded and exited, closing the door behind him.

"Now that he's gone," Ulysse whispered, "what do you really think caused Lindt's death?"

"Reddish color in the cheeks, petechiae in the eyes," Athenor muttered, and lowered his splayed right hand over Lindt's face, positioning it so that the nostrils were covered by the web between his thumb and forefinger, with his palms lying on the lips. His right forefinger touched the left upper eyelid and the tip of his thumb touched just below the right eye.

Ulysse exhaled slowly. "When I practiced law in Droitwijk, I once defended a murderer. He was a common robber who killed his victims. He showed me his technique – putting his hand like that over the victim's mouth and nostrils. He said it only took a minute or two to smother someone. He held his left hand behind the head, keeping it fixed so that the victim could not jerk their head away."

"It likely took far less time for an elderly man who was already half unconscious." Athenor disengaged his hand. "By the by, was your client acquitted?"

Ulysse smiled "No, he was hanged, but I collected my fee anyway." His smile faded and he glanced at the closed door. "But, why? Why would Kitzler want to kill Lindt?"

"Herbst told us Kitzler was at the scene when the ghost attacked. Why was that?"

"I understand his lodgings are immediately nearby," Ulysse began.

"But recall what Herbst said – that witnesses heard Kitzler call from the top of the *Seemansturm* and then come down to Lindt and Bierhals. What were they all doing there together?"

"A conclave of some sort," Ulysse pulled on his chin thoughtfully. "But I understand that Lindt was a patient of Kitzler's before this. He'll just say it was a medical consultation."

"At the top of the *Seemansturm* instead of here? Hardly likely. No. A conclave, I agree. But one that Kitzler wanted to keep secret."

"Should we confront him?"

"Not just yet. But he bears watching." Athenor leaned over the upturned face again and gently fingered the scratches on the eyelid and cheek. "Tch-tch, Dr. Kitzler. It seems you forgot to trim your fingernails."

14. Gerben Schreur

"I still find it all difficult to believe."

It was the third time in the last half-hour that those words escaped Mayor Schreur's scowling lips. He had removed his scratch-wig, unconcerned for the present about any embarrassment. He was in his own office in his own mansion, with only the three men seated before his desk.

He was now nervously running a hand back and forth across his bald scalp as if it would help summon a plan to avoid disaster. Fortunately for him, there were at least two minds in the room that were formulating one.

The mind of the third visitor was itself having trouble processing everything. Egon Richter squirmed in the large, cool room, momentarily distracted by the ebbing fire in the hearth at the far wall. The glow from the candelabras and chandelier brightened as, at the windows, purple dusk shaded into night.

"I'm afraid it's true, Mr. Mayor," he said apologetically. "There were many witnesses to the attack on Judge Lindt and his bailiff at the *Seemansturm*. They saw a Winter Ghost, then saw what Bierhals' corpse looked like after it was finished with him."

"The same as the tinker Felix Kikkert." Athenor could not resist reminding the sheriff of his dismissal of the tinker's death as due to exposure.

Richter winced. "As to that, I was only relying on Dr. Kitzler's opinion."

"And I understand Kitzler was also present at this attack?" Schreur fidgeted with a bowl of wilting pale roses and blue violets on his desk. At Richter's grunt of affirmation, he continued, "Has he been questioned? Especially about the cause of death this time? Or the cause of death of Judge Lindt?"

"My deputy, Herbst, visited him earlier tonight, along with these gentlemen." Richter waved at Athenor and Ulysse, who sat beside him. "Perhaps you can tell the Mayor what Kitzler said?"

"He was willing to concede that the ghost killed Bierhals," Athenor said. "He could hardly have opined otherwise, considering the many witnesses. He told us that Lindt died of natural causes…"

"A weak heart and shock," Ulysse's tone was sarcastic, but he refrained from rolling his eyes. He and Athenor had agreed to keep their suspicion about the real cause of Lindt's death to themselves for the time being.

Schreur drummed his fingers on the mahogany desk. "Any idea why the ghost attacked them? Just at random or were Lindt and Bierhals targeted?"

"An excellent question," Athenor replied. "I suspect the latter. After all, if the ghost was merely striking randomly, it could have pounced on any of those townsfolk."

"Any thoughts about why?" Schreur pursued.

Athenor hesitated before answering, unsure of how much to share with Schreur and Richter. Finally, he replied, "I think the Winter Ghosts are searching for an object here in town that poses a threat to them. I think they killed the elderly woman, Gertrude Vogt, searching for it. I think they sniffed it out near the *Seemansturm* earlier tonight."

"Do you suppose the ghosts thought that Lindt or Bierhals had this object?" Richter asked. Athenor hid his amusement at the sheriff's rapid conversion from skeptic to believer.

"When I asked Herbst whether he found anything unusual on them, he said he had searched Bierhals and found nothing. He did not search Lindt since the judge desperately needed to be taken to the clinic."

"And once Lindt arrived, did Kitzler or his staff search him?" Richter asked.

"Kitzler wouldn't answer any questions at all from Mayor von Mardure or me," Athenor replied. "By the time we arrived, Lindt was already dead. I did search through his clothing myself. Nothing."

"But we want to have Kitzler questioned further," Ulysse added. "And not just about that. About what Lindt and Bierhals were doing there at the tower in the first place. And why he himself was in the tower at the same time."

"I suppose Dr. Kitzler had a legitimate reason for being there," Schreur said cautiously. "After all, his house is at the foot of the *Seemansturm*. You seem to be implying they all were meeting together. Is there any corroboration of that?"

"No," Ulysse frowned. "Not yet at least."

"But I would also like Kitzler to answer questions about his patient, Baldur Rathenau," Athenor added. "You've been told about him, Mr. Mayor?"

"Sheriff Richter informed me just before your arrival here," Schreur replied somberly. "Monstrous enough for an inoffensive man like Rathenau to be slowly poisoned, let alone by his own wife. Has she said anything yet, Sheriff?" Richter had been obliged to reveal Baldur being poisoned but omitted that it was by ingestion of lead.

Richter shook his head. "She's in her cell. She's stubbornly silent—refuses to answer any questions at all. At this point, we don't know whether she acted alone or with an accomplice."

"Meaning we don't know if she merely hated her husband or conspired with a secret lover to eliminate him. Oreste von Mardure suggested tapping into the gossip at Baldur's church to ferret out any rumors," Athenor said. "But what I'm wondering is why Dr. Kitzler failed to accurately diagnose Baldur's ailment."

"He'll just claim to be incompetent," Ulysse said. "Which he probably is."

Schreur turned those ideas over in his mind. "And Pastor Rathenau? Will he live?"

"I think so," Athenor answered. "He likely will never recover his full health. He might improve slightly with his meals now prepared by Johanna von Mardure. But he's a broken man. When not quietly weeping, he just stares hollowly at the wall."

"My cousin will shelter him at his house for the time being," Ulysse said. "We all agreed that since Kitzler has failed him, Dr. Athenor will take over his care."

"Apart from further questioning of Kitzler, is there anything else you can suggest?" Schreur asked. "Particularly something about how to stop the ghosts?"

"The object they seek is a talisman, a gem. We've seen a drawing of it," Athenor admitted. "It must have the power to defeat or destroy them, otherwise they would not seek it so determinedly. So, we must find it before they do."

"Where would you even begin to look?" Schreur spread his hands with bewilderment.

"Three places," Athenor replied grimly. "First - that attic where the elderly Vogt woman was killed. She might have had it. Baldur said he and Bella searched there. It's just possible it's still there, or perhaps Bella took it and hid it or gave it to someone else. Second — the *Seemansturm*. Could it have been hidden there? Could it still be hidden there?" He trailed off in thought.

"And the third?" Richter asked.

"Nikolasz Schraal. Baldur said he knows more about the Winter Ghosts and this talisman than anyone."

"We tried talking to him before," Ulysse interjected. "Without any success."

"But you didn't have the law with you then," Richter smiled thinly. "When can you join Deputy Herbst in starting for Cloud Village?"

"Tomorrow, I should think. I want to look at Gertrude Vogt's garret tonight and the *Seemansturm* tomorrow morning when there's enough light. We can also question Kitzler tomorrow – with your help, Sheriff. After that, Herbst, Ulysse, and I will travel to Cloud Village."

"All right." Schreur leaned back in his chair and gazed at the windows where flickers of candlelight were reflected. "Is there anything we can do in the meantime?"

Athenor considered. "Bootless to warn people to stay inside their dwellings since the ghosts can penetrate them – as they did with that garret. Nor do I believe that there is any earthly weapon that will harm them. We must find the talisman and determine how to use it against them…" He paused. "So, at this point, my only advice would be – watch for them and pay attention to where they strike."

Both Schreur and Richter blinked with confusion. "What?" "Why?"

"Because wherever the ghosts come, there we will also likely find the talisman."

15. At the Garret

Ulysse led the way up the dark stairs to the third floor of the boarding house, holding a lantern high and muttering curses with each step. Oreste followed at his heels, picking his way carefully, and Athenor brought up the rear. Other than the sound of their footfalls and the swish of their cloaks – and Ulysse's imprecations – the building was silent.

"Have the other tenants moved out?" Athenor called ahead to Oreste's retreating shoulders. "We've not seen a soul since we entered."

"Yes. Many left here after Gertrude was killed. The rest earlier today when they heard what happened at the *Seemansturm*."

"Judging by the junk on these stairs, they left in a damnable hurry," Ulysse rasped. "Going up these stairs, I've already tripped over a raggle-taggle of spoons, boots, blankets, and a child's ugly doll. That one almost twisted my ankle - I think its face smirked at me afterward."

Both Oreste and Athenor had to stifle a chuckle. Ulysse's grumbles finally came to an end as he stepped onto the third-floor hallway and paused to catch his breath. The others came up alongside him.

Oreste peered down the darkened hall. The window at the end showed only the night sky. It was overcast, without stars. He nudged Ulysse and they went to the far end and the short series of steps leading to the garret. He produced the key to the iron padlock and opened the door. They entered and Ulysse set about lighting the several candles in the room, including one set on the windowsill above the hinged larder.

He wrinkled his nose, bent, and carefully lifted the lid to shine his light inside. "Hmph! Moldy bread and rotten vegetables."

"I've had supper already," Athenor remarked dryly. "But do you see any rats or rat droppings in there?"

Ulysse lowered the lantern inside the box and moved it back and forth. "No."

"I don't see any droppings around the rest of the room either," Oreste remarked, holding one of the candles. "Even vermin want no truck with the ghosts, it seems."

"Do you genuinely think we'll find the gem here?" Ulysse let the larder lid bang shut.

"No," Athenor replied. "I merely wanted to ensure we didn't miss something important. If the gem was still here, the ghosts would not have been at the *Seemansturm*. That's where it likely was at the time – probably no longer, though."

"So, that's why you didn't make searching the tower a priority?" Oreste asked.

Athenor nodded. "But the question remains – what was it doing there in the first place? Who took it there and do they still have it?"

He lifted another candle in its iron holder and scanned the room – the small, blanketed cot that served as a bed, the washstand, the nicked and worn wardrobe, the solitary chair near the potbelly stove, the iron trash box next to the small stack of firewood.

He felt a quiet sadness. He had not known Gertrude Vogt, but surely this was a pathetic legacy for anyone. A dismal, hardscrabble life with unending drudgery. And when the daily work was done, only a pitiful attic room in which to reflect upon her loneliness. And perhaps to finally realize the futility of whatever dreams she once might have had.

Imagine what finding a valuable gem would mean to such a person — an escape into a new and more comfortable life. No. If Gertrude had found the *Oculus Velnias*, she would not have relinquished it to Baldur. He mentioned some of this to his companions.

"Baldur said he and Bella searched this room together but didn't find it," Oreste said. "It's possible that if Gertrude found it, she sold it to a receiver before her death. Maybe she never got the chance to spend her profits."

"That's one possibility. But, if so, where is the money she received?" Athenor conceded. "Another possibility is that Bella *did* find it here but hid the fact from Baldur. Since she wanted him dead, she would scarcely have given it to him — something that Schraal told him might restore his health."

"We could search Baldur's parsonage," Oreste suggested. "It might turn up there."

"I doubt it. If it was there, why the attack at the *Seemansturm?* Assuming it was not random — and the ghosts have seemingly killed at random before — they must have sensed that the talisman was there."

"But taken there by whom?" Ulysse asked. "A receiver who was sold it by Gertrude or Bella?"

"Or someone else," Athenor mused, bending to look under the bed. "If Bella has an accomplice, they could have taken it there."

"Why would *anyone* take it there?" Ulysse asked irritably, reaching a hand into the trash box by the stove. "Here now, what's this?"

He fished out the discarded partial animal skull that Bella had tossed inside. He held it up for inspection.

"Oh, Baldur did mention that to me," Oreste said. "The petrified skull of an alligator gar. He thought Gertrude had uncovered that in the Town Hall cellar."

"Might I see that?" Athenor leaned close as Ulysse held it up with both hands. He inspected it carefully. He had fished in many a river and lake in Canada when he was in the French Colonial Marines and had caught several gars. Not many — they were poor eating. But he knew what a clean-picked gar skull looked like, and this was not one. Yes, it had a long snout, but the head was broader, and at the front of the upper jaw there was a long, curving fang. Gars had no such scimitar-like fangs. But he let his thoughts trail away. There were more important considerations at present. He waved a dismissive hand and Ulysse promptly dumped the fossil back into the trash-box.

"So, again." Ulysse continued, "Why would the talisman be at the tower, do you think?"

"Probably a hiding place," Athenor answered. "But why that particular place, I can't guess."

"And where do Lindt, Bierhals, or Kitzler fit into all that? The ghost attacked because it sensed the gem – at that time, anyway," Ulysse continued. "Since it attacked Lindt and Bierhals, and not Kitzler, do you suppose they had it on their persons?"

"That would make sense. Assuming Lindt had it, he might have been wanting to sell it to Kitzler," Athenor mused. "I can imagine Kitzler wanting it for his medical practice if it genuinely had any restorative power. And I can also imagine him murdering Lindt to avoid paying or to keep his secret."

Ulysse rubbed his jaw. "If Lindt had it, that suggests he got it from a receiver. Being a judge, he came into contact with numerous criminal elements."

"Or he might have gotten it from Bella," Athenor suggested. "He was a member of her husband's congregation, after all. They knew each other."

Oreste snorted. "Surely, Seth, you aren't suggesting that Bella and Lindt were…involved with each other?"

"The judge was not only old but decrepit. I don't see a woman as attractive as Bella choosing him over more appealing paramours. But she still could have consigned him the gem, knowing those criminal contacts he had." Athenor shook his head to clear it. "But all this speculation is pointless. What matters is the current location of the gem.

"The last suspected location was at the *Seemansturm* – unless Kitzler found it on Lindt while…er…doctoring him.

In either case, our next step is searching the tower – although it's probably useless."

"And Kitzler?" Ulysse asked. "Richter said he would question him and invited us to be present."

"I have little hope of eliciting anything from him except denials and evasions. If he has the gem, he's probably hidden it elsewhere." Athenor said doubtfully. "I think we will only get our true answers from the one person who knows the most about this business."

"Schraal?" Ulysse smiled grimly. "Do you think he'll be more pliable to questioning than Kitzler? Even with Deputy Herbst along?"

"No. But we must try. More than anyone, he has a desire for the *Oculus Velnias*. Regardless of who first unearthed it or whatever hands it passed through, it would likely find its way to him in the end." Athenor hesitated, "And what that end might be, I dread to guess."

16. Nathan's Return

Storm clouds had chased Alistair Nathan on Hop-Toad Road all the way back from *Kùmhòkunk*. By tomorrow, they would reach Loreley, he thought. And by that time, he would be safely at his own modest rooming house, catching up on his sleep. Some other nurse would have to man the Kitzler Clinic tomorrow.

The Loreley Courthouse clock was showing eleven o'clock when Nathan's weary horse entered the north end of town and circled the *Seemansturm* to Kitzler's nearby house. It was a handsome three-story structure with the typical extruded black grid across the outer walls, a balcony above the front porch, and another balcony above that for the third story which had four triangular gables facing each point of the compass.

Nathan swung down from the saddle and took a moment to stretch the ache from his back. He shook himself and then proceeded to the front door, using the brass knocker. At length, the door swung inward and Dr. Kitzler quickly ushered him inside. Kitzler spared a moment to furtively glance to see if anyone was around. He shut the door and led Nathan from the entranceway into the sitting room, where logs in a large brick hearth were popping and crackling. There was no other light in the room.

Kitzler adjusted his dressing robe and plucked at his mustache. He seated himself in an armchair but when Nathan began to do likewise, waved an impatient hand. "You won't be staying that long, Alistair. Just tell me what Schraal said."

Nathan frowned at the discourteousness. Not that he wanted to stay any longer than necessary. He briefly relayed Schraal's acceptance of the offer and that the pastor would arrive at the clinic sometime tomorrow.

Kitzler visibly relaxed and did not reply for a moment, then: "Very good, Alistair. Very good."

"Would you mind telling me what it's all about, sir?" Nathan was not usually one to inquire about his employer's business, but he was tired and irritable from the trip and still nettled by Schraal's rudeness.

"What?" Kitzler shook himself from his reverie. "Oh, just a business transaction. You did leave my letter with Schraal? He did not tell you the contents, did he?"

"Yes, to the first and no to the second." Nathan hesitated. "Forgive me. It was just a long trip to Cloud Village and back. And not a relaxing one – with the Winter Ghosts on the prowl again."

Kitzler inspected him narrowly. "Did you see them?"

"No. But everyone in town is alarmed after what happened to Judge Lindt and his bailiff. And…er…disturbed by the tales spreading about Bella Rathenau." He dropped his eyes with embarrassment, remembering his suspicions about her visits to Kitzler.

"What have you heard about that?" Kitzler tried to seem casual, but in truth, he had been silently consumed by that news all day. Not that he was concerned for Bella – only that she might implicate him.

Nathan shuffled his feet. "Not more than anyone else. That she's in gaol accused of trying to poison her husband."

"I think that will be difficult to prove," Kitzler advanced cautiously. "He's been a sick man for a long time. As his physician, I certainly never suspected any such thing…but I suppose I could be wrong."

"A shame if it's true, sir. My sympathies." When Kitzler arched a quizzical eyebrow, Nathan continued nervously. "Just that she was your friend and all…"

A flicker of alarm crossed Kitzler's face, quickly suppressed. "I have many friends," he replied coldly. " *Frau* Rathenau was my patient, as you well know. As was her husband, as are most folk. But…I will be happy to cooperate with the sheriff in any way I can."

"Of course, of course, sir." Nathan was squirming uncomfortably. "But if there's nothing else, I'm in sore need of sleep and…"

"Forgive my obtuseness," Kitzler rose and steered him back into the entranceway. "But I wonder, Alistair, if I could impose on you one last thing…"

Nathan waited while the physician opened the front door and guided him outside. "Can you sleep at the clinic tonight? You can take the examining room closest to my office – I've had the bed freshly made up."

When Nathan blinked with puzzlement, Kitzler went on, "Just with everything happening and that vile Schraal coming tomorrow…I would just feel more at ease if there was someone I trust there. Not that you would need to be on duty tonight. Nurse Blanchard is already at his post. I want you there just in case Schraal decides to pay a visit and steal what I've offered to sell."

Nathan returned him a doubtful look but nodded. Kitzler clapped him on the shoulder and watched as he remounted his horse and trotted off down the lane.

Kitzler watched him go until he vanished into the darkness. True enough that Schraal might try to burglarize his clinic tonight. But the main reason was that he had moved the gem from the *Seemansturm* earlier that night to the clinic. That would make it easier to complete the transaction with Schraal tomorrow. But more importantly, if the ghosts smelled out its track and found it there, they would be far away from his house. As for Nathan and Blanchard? Well, nurses were replaceable – as replaceable as lovers like Bella.

But he did need to firm up his defense should that deceitful and useless *sau* betray him. He had little to worry about, though. Even if it was established that they had been secret lovers, it would only be her word against his that he helped with her murder plan. And who would believe an unfaithful murderess?

Yet, Richter was bound to question him, at least about his treatment of Baldur. He certainly did not want the sheriff to interview him at the clinic. What if he was there when Schraal arrived? No. Better to go to the Sheriff's Office instead. That would also give the appearance of an innocent man cooperating with the authorities. Yes, that was the way to play the cards…

His thoughts were interrupted by a rustling wind that tugged at his clothes. He glanced up at the observatory atop the tower where it pierced the stars. He thought to see some of those stars momentarily blotted out as shadows passed across them to enter the open observatory and then flit back out again. He watched them with interest for a moment, then smiled slyly and returned inside his house, and quietly shut the door.

17. On Hop-Toad Road

As they pushed north along the road, a rampart of black clouds crept to meet them. Late morning sunlight began to fade. The air was pregnant with the smell of impending rain and the plain was silent except for the soft clop of their horses' hoofs and the distant murmur of wind.

Athenor rose in his stirrups to peer ahead. He thought to see movement at the bend in front, where a thicket hid the road. But the movement was not repeated, and he settled down in the saddle.

"Something, Doctor?" Georg Herbst asked nervously, fingering the butt of the pistol at his belt.

Athenor gave a slight shrug. On the other side of him, Ulysse craned to squint ahead and remarked, "I don't see anything…and for that, I'm glad."

They kneed their horses and plodded on. They had not spoken much since leaving Loreley. But they were all still brooding about that morning's inquiries – and how they had come up dry.

"Did you believe anything that twistical[24] Kitzler said?" Ulysse's question encompassed both of his companions. Before Athenor could reply, Herbst blurted out,

"Not a word! I've been a sheriff's deputy for years. I know when someone's lying. But then" he trailed off, "I

____

[24] Slang for dishonest

don't see how you could prove it. The man was as smooth as owl-shite."

They had all been present at Richter's office when Kitzler had surprisingly appeared for an interview that morning. Athenor and Ulysse had just returned from a fruitless search of the *Seemansturm*. They had listened quietly while Kitzler claimed he had merely happened to be at the tower for a breath of air when Lindt and Bierhals were attacked. Yes, those witnesses that saw Lindt and Bierhals emerging from the tower before they were attacked were correct. But it had just been a coincidence they were all there at the same time – no meeting had been planned. He had no idea why they were there.

When Athenor had abruptly asked if he knew anything about the *Oculus Velnias*, Kitzler had blinked and too quickly replied, "No! Er…what's that? I don't know what you're talking about." Herbst had also noticed that reaction and filed it away.

Richter seemingly had not noticed and resumed his questioning. But as he did, Athenor found himself wondering if the gem had passed through Kitzler's hands and if that was the reason why he had murdered Lindt – perhaps to steal it from the judge. If so, was it in Kitzler's possession now – hidden somewhere? Or had it already reached Nikolasz Schraal, who most fervently wanted it? He had hoped he would find out when they arrived at Cloud Village.

When Richter had turned to the issue of Baldur's medical treatment, Kitzler had recovered his composure. The sheriff told him only that Bella had been poisoning her husband – not revealing the type of poison used. Kitzler admitted that he had missed any sign of poisoning and professed that he felt bad that he had failed his patient.

"So, your defense is that you're inept?" Ulysse had mocked.

It was gratifying to see Kitzler forced to swallow that humiliation in silence. But it had annulled further inquiry on that topic. Richter then switched his questions to Bella and asked if he had had any suspicions about what she was doing.

Kitzler had been too shrewd to cast aspersion onto her, which an accomplice might have done. He only claimed ignorance of any such scheme and hoped that the terrible allegation was not true, but that he had confidence in Richter to ferret out the truth. That had seemed to mollify the sheriff, but Athenor had wondered that if Kitzler had no hesitation about murdering Lindt, he likely would have none about helping murder Baldur, too. But he said nothing, content to wait upon Oreste to elicit gossip linking Kitzler and Bella. But even if such gossip supported a romantic linkage, he thought sourly, Kitzler could still plausibly deny involvement in the attempted murder.

Oh, Herr Doktor, you are one conniving and cunning bastard! Athenor thought at the time.

But he forced such memories from his mind. There were more important issues at stake. Baldur could give them no further information about the Winter Ghosts. There was only one person who could – Schraal. Or maybe…maybe there was one other person at Cloud Village. If she – and Hans Martens – were willing…

They rounded the bend and saw the side road leading off to the woods where the ruins of the haunted lodge stood. As they passed by the path, they all turned to look. Not far distant were the remnants of Kikkert's wagon, still strewn about the long, newly-green grasses. A large portion of the canvas cover tilted up on its hoop, blocking the view behind it.

Athenor crossed himself, still feeling guilty that he had initially not thought to mourn the tinker. Ulysse quickly imitated him with embarrassment. Herbst was seemingly indifferent, or perhaps he was merely absorbed in his thoughts.

They all trotted up the road and their figures dwindled and vanished into the lowering black ocean of cloud. Rain was starting to patter down on the dusty road. Drops tapped onto the debris of the wagon on the side road as a horse and rider emerged from behind the blocking canvas.

Nikolasz Schraal pulled his cloak tighter about him and tugged his slouch hat firmer onto his brow. One hand was on the reins, the other fingered two objects hanging from his belt. A small money-pouch. And the hilt of a sheathed *khukuri* knife.

He guided his horse onto Hop-Toad Road and turned it south in the direction of Loreley Town. He spared a glance backward along the road and sighed, wondering if he would miss Cloud Village or the East Wind Reformed Church there.

He did not expect to see either again.

18. Schraal's Plan

Although it was only early afternoon, the storm made it seem dark as midnight at Cloud Village. Icy rain lashed down on the rooftops and at the few tribespeople scurrying through the mud. Inside the East Wind Reformed Church, there were several congregants at their prayers, either by intention or as an excuse to shelter there. Assistant Pastor Gabriël Martens was sitting in the front pew, speaking with an elderly couple when the doors opened, and three men staggered in from the rain.

All eyes turned as they stamped their feet dry and Athenor and Ulysse respectfully removed their slouch hats. Herbst only wore a shako, useless for the rain, but had pulled his cloak atop it. He now shrugged the cloak down and looked around sheepishly.

Gabriël disengaged himself from the couple with apologies and approached the three, worry writ on his face.

"Is there unwelcome news of some kind?" His question was directed at Herbst.

"None that concerns your village," the deputy answered. "We're here to see Pastor Schraal."

"He's not here. He rode out some time ago, said he was going to Loreley on some business." His brow puckered with puzzlement. "Surely you must have met him on the road?"

Athenor frowned. So, he had seen someone at the bend after all. "We seem to have missed him. But, since we are here, we'd like to inspect his study…"

"To see anything he might have written about the Winter Ghosts," Ulysse said impatiently. His small figure seemed even more shrunken by being soaked.

"By the by," Athenor continued, "has anyone from Loreley visited him lately?"

Gabriël hesitated, as if afraid to betray a confidence, then considered the intensity of the physician's stare. "Yes, last night." He told them about Alistair Nathan's visit, including how the nurse had delivered a letter from Athaulf Kitzler, and how the pastor had told him the doctor's terms were "acceptable." And that he agreed to meet Kitzler at his clinic the following day – which was today. "I hope our pastor is not in any trouble…"

"Not as much as Kitzler," Ulysse rasped, turning to Athenor. "So, he found it after all."

"And wasted no time in trying to sell it," Athenor said grimly. "But at least we know where it is…for the present."

"The Kitzler Clinic?" Herbst asked. "Shouldn't we be starting back then? Maybe we can get there in time to stop the sale."

"You may go, Georg," Athenor replied. "Mayor von Mardure and I still have some things that bear investigation here."

Herbst hesitated. "Our horses need some rest first. I'll stay until you both leave." But Athenor suspected the deputy was wary about traveling the road alone.

He gave Herbst a brief nod and then returned to Gabriël. "Can you show us into the parsonage, Pastor Martens?"

Gabriël swallowed nervously and bobbed his head. He led them back through the chancel to the vestry and the simple wooden door leading to the parsonage. He had lit a candle from one in the sanctuary and now used it to guide them through a small sitting room to the back study.

Athenor scanned Schraal's dismal quarters and found them almost as pathetic as Gertrude Vogt's. There were only smoldering ashes in the brick hearth, no paintings or decorations on the walls, and a couple of rough chairs. There was a small kitchenette with cupboards and a hinged larder. Two doorways were at the rear. Gabriël directed them toward the right-hand one. Athenor supposed the other led to a bedchamber. It all looked as neglected and cheerless as the inside of a cave, as if its occupant had all but withdrawn from human society.

Gabriël lit the several candles in the study but that did not completely dispel the shadows crouching in the corners.

"Will you need me for anything else?"

"I wonder if you would permit us – me, at least – to speak with Cholena and Hans."

Gabriël hesitated, then nodded gravely. "I'll go and ask Cholena. I know Hans is at home with her now, what with the storm. Whether or not she agrees, I can't guarantee."

"Understood. If she can tell us anything to help defeat the ghosts that would be most helpful."

Gabriël smiled weakly and went out, leaving the three alone. As Ulysse and Athenor began to look at the papers, scrolls, and books piled on the desk, Herbst excused himself and retired to the sitting room. "I will leave you to it. I'll see about a fire."

"We won't be here that long," Ulysse called out to his retreating form.

"Let be, Ulysse," Athenor whispered. "I think our friend is discomfited by this room. And I don't blame him. Some rooms retain a sinister aura shed by their inhabitants. This seems one of them."

"You're right, Seth. If ever a room was less like that of a pastor, it's this." Ulysse edged away from the desk and almost bumped into the wall behind it where the animal skull was fastened. He flinched with surprise. "Damn me, I thought I'd seen the last of you in the garret."

Athenor turned from where he sat and inspected the skull. "Curious. Another one but more complete than the other. And not something of any beauty to warrant a wall mounting."

"Oreste thought the one in Gertrude's trash box was something she found in the ruined foundation of Town Hall. Where did this one come from, do you suppose?" He ran a tentative finger along the jaw. "Fossilized as well."

Athenor shook his head and returned to the desk, sifting through a stack of papers. His eye fell upon the one where

Schraal had penciled his remarks and examined them with interest. After a few minutes, he motioned Ulysse to his side and showed them to him.

"…Hop-Toad Road," Ulysse read slowly. "…The road that ended in the middle of Loreley. Drögö knew where he was going. Of all the roads in this world, this must be the one."

"You remember the inscription in that drawing Baldur showed us? The Dungeon of the Angels? Where The Road Ends?" Athenor said meditatively. "I've always thought the last phrase was just metaphorical. But what if it was literal? A map to where the Dungeon is located?"

"So that ancient foundation in Loreley…that was once the Dungeon? Not in Asia or the Lower Americas? But here?"

"Schraal thinks so, and he's doubtless right," Athenor replied. "And he believes that Drögö came here from Moravia and Wallachia searching for it – and for the gem that once empowered its guardian, *Velnias*. And what could his intention have been except to open the gate and let loose the imprisoned evil angels?"

"Maybe the Children of the Storm killed him before he could."

"Maybe. But is that *Schraal's* intention, too?" Athenor contemplated. "If so, I cannot see how he could hope to control them. Or persuade them to kill the Storm Children on his behalf. No. We don't fully understand Schraal's plan yet."

"In any case, I think we should return to Loreley immediately and stop that damnable fool."

Athenor considered, then replied. "You and Georg go. I still need to try to talk with Cholena to see if she can tell me what we need to know – should we fail to stop Schraal in time."

Ulysse's mouth twisted with dread. He bobbed his head and rushed into the sitting room where he exchanged a quick word with Herbst and together they went back into the vestry. Athenor was left alone with his thoughts.

He spent several more minutes sifting through the various papers and sketches on the desk. He found a drawing of the *Oculus Velnias* identical to the one Baldur had shown them – a black, lusterless gem set in a rectangular iron mounting with arcane symbols. He noticed several iron-bound books laying open, one atop another. The pages of the first few were merely faded Latin texts. Others showed woodcuts of demons of various types – some in the form of birds, snakes, toads, and others of more humanoid aspect.

When he turned a page, he saw a woodcut with a familiar name – *Velnias* – along with a depiction of the three-headed guardian of the underworld prisons. He had never seen it before now.

So this was *Velnias*. She had a squat body with six crooked legs on either side and three serpentine heads that writhed on long necks. The elongated jaws were filled with saw-like teeth and two curving fangs like scimitars. In the forehead of the central head was the rectangular dark gem – the *Oculus Velnias*.

Athenor studied the drawing with interest. He now understood what animal skull was fastened to the wall in Schraal's study and what Gertrude had found in the rubble. But where was the third skull?

He closed the book and set it aside. Beneath it was another book, open to a page with a color painting. It appeared to be that of an ancient shepherd, sitting on a stump and leaning with both hands upon a crooked staff. He wore a tall, broad-brimmed conical hat that threw a shadow onto his face. From within that shadow, two eyes glimmered like red coals above a predatory nose and a mirthless smile. He was dressed in a coarse brown robe that came to the ankles. Those ankles ended in goat-like hoofs.

Below this painting was written, *ÖRDÖG*. And under that, *Daemonium Dacium.*

Athenor narrowed his eyes and closed the book. He slowly rose and exited the study to find a breathless Gabriël entering the sitting room from the vestry.

"Doctor, has anything happened? I just saw your friends making for the stables. They said they needed to return to town right away…Did you still…?"

"Yes. I'd still like to speak with Cholena if she and your brother are willing."

"When I asked them together, Hans spoke for her again. She said…" Gabriël hesitated, *"Yes. Fetch him to me. There is not much time left."*

Athenor motioned him forward and he turned and led the way. They proceeded in silence through the vestry, down the aisle of the nave, and out the door. They trudged silently through the muddy lanes in the downpour. To the south, there flashed sheet lightning across the blackness, followed by distant mutters of thunder.

Eventually, they arrived at Gabriël's two-story cottage. In the sitting room, a fire in the stone hearth threw welcome light and heat into all but the shadowed corners. Athenor and the deacon deposited their cloaks and hats on pegs next to the door, and Gabriël ushered the physician up the narrow stairs next to the hearth.

The warmth from the fireplace pervaded the upper hallway and the two open doors along it. As they passed the first, Athenor glimpsed twin beds, where he presumed the brothers slept. They entered the second doorway into a neat cedar-lined room with a single window that was gray with rain. A comfortable-looking bed was situated beneath it, and a rocking chair was beside it.

In that chair was an elderly woman in Native raiment – an ankle-length fringed robe with bright, decorative patterns, moccasins, and a feathered shawl. Her white hair retreated from her wrinkled brow and a single braid curled around her neck and onto her breast. Bright brown eyes were buried amid a nest of wrinkles, but there was a serene smile at her lips – although there was some flattening of the right nasolabial fold and a droop at the right corner of the lip. Athenor remembered what Gabriël had said about her attack of apoplexia.

At her feet, leaning against the side of the rocking chair, Hans was also rocking back and forth in a matching rhythm.

His eyes were vacant, and his mouth hung slackly open, from which drooled a soft, repetitive, "No, no, no."

Athenor slowly approached and knelt on the other side of the chair, meeting the woman's eyes. He began, "Mistress Cholena, I'm honored you've chosen to speak with me."

Her smile widened to the extent that was possible. She did not speak, but suddenly Hans stopped rocking and stiffened, his eyes rolling up. He spoke fluently in English with intelligence and eloquence:

"Nikolasz plans a very dangerous thing. He hates the Thunder-Beings, *Pèthakhue* and his children. He hates them so much that he would risk the destruction of us all. He will return the gem to *Velnias* and she will live again – but not to resume her former duties.

"All that I know has been imparted to me by Nikolasz, who learned it from his books and scrolls. In exchange, I told him all I knew and remembered about the Thunder-Beings, not realizing what he intended.

"You know of the Dungeon at the end of Hop-Toad Road? Long ago, an evil angel who was not imprisoned sought to free his incarcerated brethren by removing the gem of *Velnias*, her third eye. That weakened her enough for him to sever her three heads. Like his brethren and *Velnias*, he had a fleshly form. They were not pure spirits at that time.

"So, he flattered and seduced her into relaxing her guard, plucked out the gem from her forehead, and proceeded to cut off all her heads, one by one. But even the quickest sword could not decapitate them all in time. As the last stroke fell, one severed head snapped its jaws onto him and slew him.

"His spirit left his body and wailed with despair. For the stone gateway of the Dungeon had collapsed into rubble and buried the gem and the three severed heads of the serpent-being. Those evil angels inside have been imprisoned ever since."

"But this murderous angel did not excavate the gem?"

"How could he? No intangible spirit hands could lift tons of rubble or grasp the gem. No, he needed to acquire a human body, a host he could possess. At that time, there were few humans in the world, and none of them on this continent yet. So, the demon spirit fled back across the world to his home – a lonely, ancient shrine – and there waited for a suitable human. But few dared to visit the ruins of his haunted shrine because it was guarded by poisonous vapors.

"So, he waited many thousands of years, saw the coming of the Dacians, the Romans, the Slavs and Bulgarians, the Mongols, and finally the Turks and their Suzerainty of Wallachia. The ancient Romans that conquered Dacia learned of him and recorded his name, but gave his shrine a wide berth.

"Yes, he waited through all the successors of Rome for his intended host, for he wanted a human whose soul was tainted and suitable for housing his spirit. A human who was willing to brave the poison fumes and climb down into the lowest recess of the shrine.

"Finally, Mátyás Sovány came, already a delver into dark secrets, his Christian faith gone by that time, replaced by diabolism. And with that evil magic, he guarded himself against the poisonous vapors. When he arrived at the deep heart of the shrine, the demon spirit possessed his willing body.

"And once having possessed him, this ancient demon spirit wore human flesh to become the sorcerer Lurkó Drögö – at last with physical hands able to excavate the gem and to use its power. Over time, there developed other physical changes in the possessed body of Sovány as well…

"But even so, Drögö failed. He did not recover the gem before the Winter Ghosts killed him. The gem lay buried until now. But he did recover one of the severed serpent heads from the rubble and kept it in his manse as a trinket to mock."

Athenor realized this was the "fossil" that Baldur said Drögö had found in the ruins. "So, Drögö planned to use the gem's power to unlock the Dungeon?"

"Yes, by empowering himself. Even separated from *Velnias*, it could empower a different supernatural creature – such as the evil angel that slew her, even in the possessed body of Sovány, which was no longer human. But it cannot empower an ordinary human at all."

"So Schraal lied to Baldur when he claimed the gem could cure him." Athenor scowled. "Then, if it cannot empower him, how could it be of any use to Schraal either? What does he plan for it?"

"He wants to revive *Velnias* by placing the gem back into the forehead of the third skull – the one in the White Lodge." Hans paused his communication as Cholena seemed to gather her thoughts, then continued, "Many ancient legends have long told of an instinctive rivalry between different supernatural beings. Some eastern European legends, which name her *Veles* or *Vélinas*, also speak of her enmity with their version of the Thunder-Beings, *Perkûnas*. Likewise, our Lenape legends tell us that the Thunder-Beings and the old serpent which we call *Maxákâk* are sworn enemies. And what can *Maxákâk* be but another name for what is called *Velnias?*

"Nikolasz hopes that by awakening her, she will destroy the Thunder-Being and his children. The Winter Ghosts know this. That is why they seek the gem to prevent it."

"And after she destroys them?" Athenor asked hesitantly. "Will she return to be Warden of the Dungeon?"

"Afterward…Woe! Woe! Woe!"

She started trembling and could not communicate for a few minutes. At her feet, Hans trembled in harmonic sympathy.

"No, nor do I think she will release the imprisoned angels. I believe she hates them and the one that slew her," Cholena finally replied through Hans. "But I fear she is so angered by her betrayal and murder that a resurrected *Velnias* will become a menace to all that lives.

"It is truly said: Take care when you enlist one monster to defeat another, lest the second prove worse than the first."

Gabriël, standing silent through all this, stared aghast at Cholena.

Cholena leaned back and her chin fell upon her chest from exhaustion. Hans shook himself from his spell and flinched as the window rattled with rain, and thunder crashed overhead. His eyes darted aimlessly in terror as he chattered out his familiar palilalia, "No, no, no." But to Athenor's ear, it sounded more like Cholena's exclamation of dread,

"Woe! Woe! Woe!"

19. A Bargain is Concluded

The storm arrived in Loreley Town earlier that day around noon, pouring gusts and rain onto the green rooftops and turning the crooked lanes into muddy streams. Inside the Kitzler Medical Clinic, Nurse Humphrey Kellett wandered from around his reception desk into the waiting room to toss another chunk of wood into the potbelly stove in the corner. Outside was the creak and rattle of the sign hanging above the front door. He was just closing the stove when that door burst open, admitting a cloaked figure amid a blast of rain.

The figure hurried inside and slammed the door shut. The few patients waiting – a mother and sick child, a rheumy oldster – were startled, but then shrank back in their chairs. The newcomer stamped his feet and shook out his sodden cloak, strewing rainwater everywhere. He lifted the broad brim of his slouch hat to glare at Kellett.

"Do you have a rain blanket for my horse?" he asked angrily. Deerskin blankets were commonplace in those times, to protect horses during a shower when not in their stables.

Kellett blinked, recognizing the man. "I'm sorry, Pastor Schraal. We have none here. Most folk in town pack them behind their saddle."

"Never mind," Schraal grunted irritably. "I won't be here that long anyway. Did Kitzler tell you to expect me?"

"Yes, sir. He is in his office waiting for you." Kellett gestured toward the hallway door. He now wished that Nurse Blanchard had not gone home at dawn, the end of his shift.

Schraal clamped his lips tightly, went to the door, and flung it open. Kellett watched him stride determinedly down the hallway. He was about to call out to ask him to be quiet because Nurse Nathan was asleep in one of the examining rooms but thought better of it. As the hallway door closed behind Schraal's retreating form, Kellett puttered around the waiting room, reluctant to approach any nearer to the hallway.

Athaulf Kitzler was sitting at his desk, wearing a white linen shirt with long sleeves and a waistcoat. He drummed his fingers and silently congratulated himself on his performance in Richter's office that morning. All except his startled reaction to the question about the gem. He had not been prepared for that, nor had imagined Athenor knew about it. In retrospect, he deduced that Baldur must have told him. Still, apart from Bella, no one else knew it was in his possession – except for Lindt and Bierhals, who were not in any position to disclose that.

But Bella…What if she betrayed him? The best course would be to deny all knowledge of the gem, regardless of what she confessed. But it might pay dividends to visit her in gaol and privately reassure her of his love, which hopefully would incentivize her to keep quiet about him. But any lawyer he hired for her would cost money – money he did not want to waste on that adulterous bitch. Damn it all! Why had he ever succumbed to her advances? That poor idiot Baldur. If he only realized he had not seduced Bella – it had been the other way around…

His reverie was interrupted by a hammering on the door, and he leaped halfway from his chair. Without waiting for his acknowledgment, the door banged open to admit Schraal. The pastor doffed his hat and shook it out onto the floor and then replaced it upon his head.

"Where is it?" he demanded, approaching the desk.

Kitzler regained his composure but remained wary. "It's here. Where is the money? The £500 I quoted you."

Schraal reached beneath his cloak and produced a small leather bag that he flung contemptuously onto the desk. Kitzler carefully opened its drawstring to pour out some coins. He quickly sifted through them and then glared at the pastor.

"There isn't £500 here. I count less than 100."

"It's all I have left. When I left Heidelberg, I only inherited a small amount, £1000," Schraal returned the glare. "I spent almost all of it on rare books and folios over the years."

"Hmph!" Kitzler snorted. "My practice alone earns me about £100 per month. This is hardly a fair exchange for the gem."

Schraal narrowed his eyes and spoke softly. "The gem does you no good. Neither you nor anyone else. It's only of use to me. You'd be wise to sell it to me at whatever price I pay and get it off your hands…before the Winter Ghosts sniff it out."

"Maybe," Kitzler replied coolly, his mind racing. "Or maybe I could sell it to you for your miserable £100 and something else…" He smiled slyly, and when Schraal did not respond, went on, "If this gem enables you to control the ghosts through whatever incantations you've learned, you could do me a favor…"

"Such as?"

"Sending the ghosts to kill someone for me." Kitzler winked. "Someone currently in the town gaol."

"I have no such power over the ghosts, with or without the gem."

"Then, perhaps you can find a way to do the job yourself." Kitzler's smile broadened. *Yes, Bella certainly could be visited by a pastor of her faith. And during that visit, Schraal might find that his hand fitted nicely over her nostrils and mouth in a way I could teach him…*

"I have no time to waste, even if I wanted to be your assassin," Schraal moved to the physician's elbow. "I'm here now and I want the gem – *now*."

Kitzler, still wrapped in his scheming thoughts, did not notice the menace purring behind the pastor's words. *Maybe if I toy with this dolt a little, I can pressure him…* "Well, if you can't do as I ask, then I'm afraid we have no bargain."

He reached out to contemptuously shove the spilled coins away. Scarcely had his fingertips touched them when a blade flashed and the tip of a steel *khukuri* skewered the back of his hand, pinning it to the desk. He gazed dumbly as Schraal leaned on the hilt of the knife. Then, as his shocked senses began to feel the pain, he opened his mouth to scream.

Schraal clapped his other hand over the physician's mouth, ripped the knife from the hand, and put the tip to his throat.

"I don't want to kill you, Kitzler," he whispered fiercely. "I don't need a party of men chasing me when I ride to… my destination. But I will…unless you tell me where the gem is hidden."

Eyes goggling with pain and fright, Kitzler jerked his head to the wall behind him. Schraal lifted his gaze to the framed sheepskin diploma proclaiming UNIVERSETEIT LEIDEN. He smiled cynically and removed his hand from Kitzler's mouth but kept the knife at his throat.

Kitzler whimpered, in intense pain but afraid of crying out. Schraal scrabbled with his free hand on the desk and grabbed up the empty money pouch. Crumpling it, he shoved it into Kitzler's mouth, seized him by the shoulder, and threw him to the floor face-down. While the physician moaned and his bleeding hand twitched, Schraal used the knife to cut strips from the sleeves of his linen shirt and bound him – first around the mouth and tied at the neck, then his hands behind his back. He did not want to kill him before he found the gem.

Satisfied, Schraal smiled grimly and rose, still holding the *khukuri*. He went to the diploma and thought for a minute about simply taking it down from the wall. Then, angered at what Kitzler had forced him to do, he slashed crisscross along the diploma and then ripped the shreds from the frame.

Clinging to one of them was a strip of gummed bandage or *sparadrapum*[25] bulging with something underneath. Carefully, Schraal peeled away the sticky bandage and held the *Oculus Velnias* up to his avid eyes.

He gazed at it for a long time. He did not dare touch his finger to the black jewel that was without luster or gleam. It was flat, without facets, and the rectangular iron mounting was similarly drab, as of something that had been buried for untold millennia.

Finally, expelling his breath slowly, he gingerly placed it into a waistcoat pocket and sheathed the *khukuri* that had dangled absently from his other hand.

He scarcely glanced at Kitzler's prone and still-groaning form or the blood pooling from his hand. He stifled a chuckle. He decided Kitzler was not worth killing.

"Well, *Herr Doktor*, I hope you're adept at performing surgeries one-handed."

He glanced briefly at his coins, where they were spilled across the desk. He shook his head. *I won't need money anymore. Or anything else. I have no illusions about surviving – afterward. But it will all be worth it…*

He stepped across Kitzler, restraining an urge to kick him, and went to open the door and step into the hallway.

Nothing. No sounds of alarm. The door to Kitzler's office was solid and thick, the better to hide any sounds of his infamous amorous activities.

---

[25] A pre-industrial surgical "tape," which was first used in the 1400s to hold gauzes and wound dressings in place.

As he passed the door to one of the examining rooms, he heard someone snoring inside and chuckled to himself. When he emerged back into the waiting room, he paused to glance at Nurse Kellett sitting at the reception window.

"Dr. Kitzler told me he did not want to be disturbed for the next hour," he said sternly.

Kellett blinked, intimidated, and just bobbed his head. The other patients in the room did not react. Schraal assumed they were used to long waits for *Herr Doktor*. And by the time they discovered him, the pastor would be long gone — to the last place any would think to search for him, he hoped.

He opened the front door and stepped out into the rain, then closed it behind. He stood for a moment, staring up at the churning black clouds as a sheet of lightning turned the rain all to silver for an instant. As the thunder subsided, he thought he heard a faint singing drifting down. He shook a defiant fist at the clouds, mounted his horse, and trotted through the mud lane toward Hop-Toad Road.

20. Kitzler is Caught Out

The courthouse clock was showing three o'clock when Ulysse and Herbst rode into Loreley. The downpour continued, making it hard to see more than fifty feet in any direction. It was not surprising that they missed Schraal on his northward journey along Hop-Toad Road. If they saw him at all, he was indistinguishable from the other few travelers in that curtain of rain.

They splashed through the muddy lanes to arrive at the Office of the Sheriff. Several horses were in an adjacent open stables, tended by a wizened, white-haired groom. They trotted underneath the roof and swung down.

"More visitors! More visitors!" The groom muttered irritably. "I've about run out of stalls as it is."

"What's happening, Lemmerz?" Herbst handed his reins to the groom. "Why all the visitors?"

"You haven't heard then, Deputy? Dr. Kitzler has been attacked at his clinic. He's inside now, making a complaint to the sheriff."

"Attacked? By whom?"

"That Reformed pastor, Schraal. Who'd have thought it of a minister?" Lemmerz shook his head doubtfully.

"Did they apprehend Schraal?" Ulysse interjected as the groom led Herbst's horse inside a straw-filled stall.

"No. He left the clinic, and it wasn't until an hour later that Kitzler's nurses found him in his office, bound and gagged."

"I guess he's lucky to still be alive." Ulysse sounded disappointed. He gave over the reins of his horse to Lemmerz as he emerged from the stall.

"Does anyone know where Schraal fled?" Herbst asked, to which the groom shook his head and gestured to the front door of the Sheriff's Office. "They'll know more about it than me. I'm just a groom, thank goodness. I only have to worry about a horse bite or kick now and then, not some crazed preacher."

Herbst wasted no more time but turned and quickly walked out and around to the front door, followed by Ulysse. They hurried inside the waiting area to see Athaulf Kitzler slumped back in a chair, his face ashen, holding the wrist of his bandaged hand. Sitting beside him was Alistair Nathan, brow furrowed with worry, solicitously patting his employer on the shoulder. Standing near were Sheriff Egon Richter and Pastor Oreste von Mardure. They all glanced up as Herbst and Ulysse entered.

"You haven't seen Schraal, by any chance?" Richter asked them.

"No," Herbst replied. "He wasn't at Cloud Village when we arrived. And we didn't see him on Hop-Toad Road. But we might have missed him in this confounded rain."

"We think he might have gone to the ruins of Town Hall," Ulysse added. "Men must be sent there immediately to look for him – to stop him."

"We haven't time to explain," continued Herbst. On their ride back from Cloud Village, Ulysse had told him of what he knew about the Dungeon of the Angels and Schraal's possible plan to somehow unlock it with the *Oculus Velnias*. They had left, of course, before Athenor had talked with Cholena and had learned Schraal's true intention – to enter The White Lodge and use the gem to awaken *Velnias*.

There were two other deputies in the room, who looked questioningly at Richter, who gave them a nod of assent. They took down cloaks from beside the door and went out into the storm.

Herbst said to Richter, "We left Dr. Athenor at the village to gather more information. But he urged us to return to town with all haste and stop Schraal."

After the door was shut again, Ulysse turned to Kitzler.

"Doctor, we might not have seen Schraal at the village, but we learned a thing or two about you and…" He bent a stern gaze at Nathan, 'About you too, Alistair Nathan."

The nurse's face paled beneath his mop of sandy hair. "You know me?"

Ulysse smiled thinly. "I was a lawyer in Droitwijk Town in 1752 when Fort Saint Michael fell to that monster and saw you afterward being rebuffed by the surviving soldiers. One or two whispered some uncomplimentary things about you, Mr. Nathan. So, I wasn't surprised when Gabriël Martens told us about you delivering a missive from the good doctor here summoning Schraal to his clinic to conclude a bargain."

"What?" Richter was caught between surprise and irritation. "Dr. Kitzler, you told me that Schraal came unannounced to your clinic today, demanding opium, and when you refused, stabbed you."

Kitzler clamped his lips tightly and stared down at the floor. Nathan rose shakily to his feet, eyes wide with fright.

"All I did was convey a message from the doctor to Schraal – and return his answer."

"We know about that," Herbst interjected. "We know it was about the talisman, and that's what Dr. Kitzler here wanted to sell to Schraal. It seems the bargain didn't go as planned, eh Doctor?"

Kitzler remained mute and now closed his eyes.

"The talisman that can destroy the ghosts?" Richter asked Kitzler with suppressed anger. "You tried to sell it rather than give it to us? You put profit above the well-being of your fellow citizens?"

Kitzler made no reply.

"So, where did you get the *Oculus Velnias?*" Ulysse pursued. "From Lindt?"

"I think I can answer that." Oreste had silently followed the interchange until now. "I've made some inquiries today of the Reformed Church congregants. Some were only too eager to share their gossip – it seems Baldur is well-loved by them. And they are up in arms about the allegation against Bella. Yes, it has been rumored that she has a secret lover… And who do you suppose that is?" He smiled grimly at Kitzler.

The doctor let out a protracted sigh and addressed the floor in a low voice. "All right, yes, I was Bella's lover. She gave me the gem to sell. But I had nothing to do with her using lead to poison her husband."

At that, Richter and Ulysse exchanged a glance, for they had kept secret the type of poison used.

"Lead?" Richter's eyes glinted. "Who said anything about lead?"

Kitzler started to reply, alarm flooding his face, then fell silent.

"I seem to recall you saying something this morning about not recognizing the signs of poisoning in Baldur," Ulysse asked mockingly. "Yet, you now admit you knew it was lead poisoning. The only person who could have told you that is Bella. And that means you knew about her murder plan."

"That makes you an accessory to murder, at best. Someone who, especially being a doctor, could have stopped her or reported her," Richter said. "At worst, it makes you a co-conspirator in her murder plot — to do away with her husband so you and Bella would be free to marry."

"And if that's proven in court," Ulysse, the former lawyer, added, "You will hang alongside your beloved murderous witch."

Kitzler buried his face in his hands. Nathan had edged away from him as if fearing contagion. No one spoke for a while, then Richter motioned to Herbst.

"Deputy, kindly escort the doctor upstairs to one of our cells. Maybe the one next to Bella."

Herbst smiled thinly, went to Kitzler, and prodded him in the arm. The doctor slowly lifted his face and got to his feet, utterly deflated. He allowed Herbst to guide him down the hall toward the rear stairs, making no sound.

"What about me?" squeaked Nathan.

Richter snorted. "You're a witness at this point, nothing else. You may go, but don't leave town."

Nathan eagerly bobbed his head, took down his cloak and hat, and opened the door. No sooner had he exited than the door re-opened, and the two deputies returned.

"Anything?" Richter asked. When they both shook their heads, the sheriff turned to Ulysse.

"Now what, Mayor von Mardure? Where do we look for Schraal and that gem?"

So, I'm Mayor now, not Mister. Ulysse thought absently. He went to sit in one of the chairs, suddenly very tired. "I thought he would be in the ruins for certain. But now…I just don't know."

Oreste put a reassuring hand on his cousin's shoulder. "Perhaps Seth learned something more after you left Cloud Village."

Richter interjected with frustration, "But where *is* Dr. Athenor?"

Only the outside rumble of thunder and the sweep of the rain answered him.

21. The White Lodge

Athenor's horse raced down Hop-Toad Road, hoofs kicking up gouts of mud behind, flanks coated with sweat, tail and mane streaming back. He had been forced to use the whip, every moment fearing he would be too late to stop Schraal. But now his horse was faltering, its gallop starting to weave and stagger. Cursing freely, he eased back on the reins, slowing to a canter. If his horse died, he would have no chance at all.

At least, the rain had slackened by the time he reached the side road leading to the ruined lodge. Black clouds still churned overhead but dim red glimmers of sunset edged the jagged rampart of mountaintops to the west. Most of the storm had already moved south to Loreley.

He drew rein and dismounted as the horse continued to wobble and totter. He gave it a resigned pat on its neck and searched for something on which to secure the reins. Finding nothing, he gave up and started walking between the swishing long grass toward the woods.

He suspected that Schraal had already concluded his bargain with Kitzler and had seized the *Oculus Velnias*. But the question was – had Schraal arrived at the lodge already, or was there still time to stop him?

He had no idea what a resurrected *Velnias* might look like but suspected that its reappearance would be impossible to miss. But what if it had already been revived, and was even now headed for Loreley to lay waste to the townsfolk? What could possibly stop it? The Tornado-Being *Pèthankhue*, its ancient foe? But would even it be powerful enough?

His thoughts were interrupted by a frantic neighing behind, and he whirled to see the horse bolt off south down the road, its exhaustion forgotten, its panicked cry fading. He stood frozen for a moment, squinting to make out something coming rapidly toward him.

It was one of the Winter Ghosts. The swirling vortex was scarcely visible against the murk and the rain, but he could see the vibrating central nimbus as it came nearer, and the blue pinpointed eyes that were fastened on him.

He whipped out his pistol and fired, even though he knew it would be hopeless. After the bolt of flame and the smoke dissipated, he saw that the thing was unharmed and still racing in his direction. He made a desperate leap aside into the long, wet grass, knowing it would be futile to try to outrun it.

He waited tensely for the ghost to seize him, but only felt the rush of the whirlwind lunging past him and down the path, making the long grass spring up and writhe. Then, it was gone, and he rose to peer in astonishment as the vortex vanished into the woods.

From the direction of Hop-Toad Road behind him, there now came a hollow roar that rose and rose to a deafening pitch. He turned to see a pallid funnel inch down from the tumbling black and crimson-edged clouds and touch the ground, ripping up swathes of grass.

He froze, but the tornado did not advance toward him — nor did it move in any direction. It hovered in place, a pillar of feverishly spinning, lurid white, and for a moment he thought to see two great dark-blue eyes staring down at him.

"*Pèthankhue*," he muttered, and he imagined that it heard him. For he suddenly knew what he needed to do, although no voice had spoken to him.

He gave the tall, twisting pillar a nod of acknowledgment and rushed down the path toward the woods. He now realized that the ghost he had seen was merely fleeing its Thunder-Being father rather than trying to attack him. He was relieved – not only at that but by the realization that if the ghosts still existed then Schraal had not succeeded in awakening *Velnias*.

He hurried along the path and into the woods, while the rain steadily beat down on the tossing treetops. Finally, he debouched into the familiar glade encircled by green pine and white beech. In the center were the ruins of the White Lodge – a crumbling foundation, a jagged remnant of a back wall, and a broken, tilted chimney.

Sitting cross-legged and motionless in front of it was Schraal, seemingly like a glistening black rock in the rain. Surrounding him were the five Winter Ghosts, vibrating impatiently, hovering malevolently, but not daring to attack him. Athenor could hear their insistent wordless whispering and sensed their frustration, their hatred, their impotence. He understood that they must have been deterred by the gem, which Schraal undoubtedly possessed.

As he cautiously approached, the five ghosts turned toward him – at least, he could see their blue pinpointed eyes now. But they did not approach him, and he understood that they did not consider him a threat – unlike the man they encircled. That man now lifted his head to look at him from beneath the dripping brim of his slouch hat.

"Well, Doctor," he laughed, "If you're here, you must know about my plan. Did Cholena tell you? Her and that idiotic Hans?"

"Yes, I think I know what you intend with that third skull inside." Athenor cautiously edged closer. "Don't do it, Pastor. *Velnias* can't be trusted to kill the ghosts, and if she regains the gem, all humanity will be at risk from her murderous wrath."

"What alternative is there?" Schraal's voice was heavy with resignation. "I won't resurrect Drögö – he's too dangerous in his own right. Drögö…" He gave a weak chuckle. "Have you deduced who he truly was?"

"That painting in one of your books. I suppose I would have figured out the anagram in time anyway, but that saved me the trouble."

Schraal barked out a laugh. "Yes, yes. *Ördög* – the ancient demon of pre-Roman Dacia and all its successors, including Wallachia. The goat-footed shepherd whose sheep are naught less than people – their flesh his food and their skin his for the shearing."

"A brother to those imprisoned angels? And one who sought the gem to unlock their Dungeon when he slew *Velnias*." Athenor edged closer, wary of the hovering ghosts, whose insistent whispers and murmurs hummed with menace. "But regardless – it seems our friends here have stymied you. Are they refusing to materialize their stolen lodge?"

"Yes!" Schraal slowly rose to his feet. "They know what I intend and believe that if the lodge is not made whole, I cannot enter. And they're right! But they fear to attack me for the gem."

"I imagine their fear will ebb over time," Athenor said quietly, hesitating at the edge of the circle of ghosts. "After all, they've killed others for just being in the vicinity of the gem."

"I know." Schraal sighed deeply. "They're keeping me from leaving and over the last few hours, they have inched closer and closer."

"But there's another way to use the gem and destroy the ghosts…" Athenor began.

But then, from the direction of the path came the increasing roar of the tornado, like the voice of a thousand waterfalls. He turned to see the pallid funnel advancing slowly upon them through the woods, uprooting trees to fling them in all directions, mowing a path.

The multiple whispers of the Winter Ghosts changed to a chorus of unearthly screams and as Athenor turned back toward them, the ruins of the lodge blurred and wavered, and a ghostly mirage of the White Lodge solidified, and – suddenly it was there again. The ghastly white stone walls, the lattice-paned windows, the flat roof with its cupola, its beckoning wooden door.

The five ghosts flew up to the roof and began quickly funneling down the chimney, trying to elude the tornado *Pèthakhue*. Their father.

Schraal raced for the door, with a frightened glance back at the tornado. Athenor could scarcely blame him, as the needle tip of it — not even twenty yards in diameter — drew up in front of the lodge and stopped. Its roar had diminished, and its rotary force slowed, although the lightning forked in the high tumbling clouds overhead and the thunder crashed down.

Athenor knew that it meant no harm to him but lost no further time in chasing after Schraal, desperate to stop him before he reached the third skull. He burst through the front door which the pastor had not bothered to latch.

He found himself in the debris-filled sitting room with its two doors in the rear wall, one leading to the kitchen. In several corners were scattered bones, including several human skulls.

But when he heard quick footsteps from the second door, he rushed there and up the curving stone staircase to the second floor. He guessed that Schraal was not familiar with the layout of the house and had spent fruitless minutes searching through the human bones for the last skull.

Now, he heard a door bang open on the second floor and a strangled gasp. He reached the top of the stairs and the long hallway that stretched back to the iron spiral staircase. There were three doors on the right side and a line of rain-streaked windows on the left.

Schraal had just slammed the first door shut and recoiled, panting. On the other side, there came a frenzied hammering, and the door began to bulge out. Schraal threw Athenor a terrified look.

"They've come down the chimney in there!" Then, as he saw Athenor draw out his scramasax knife, he turned and bolted into the second room and hurriedly shut the door behind him.

Athenor did not relish the idea of killing Schraal, but realized he had to stop him any way he could. He lifted the latch of the second door, surprised to find it unlocked, and kicked it open. He darted inside to find himself in a kind of book-lined library or study.

He did not have time to notice anything else before he caught a sudden movement in the corner of his eye. Instinctively, he flung the scramasax up to his left in time to catch the downward swipe of a 10-inch-bladed *khukuri*. Blue sparks blazed at the clang of steel and Athenor was shoved off-balance by the force of Schraal's blow. He fell onto one knee, but still brought up his knife at guard, expecting another attack.

But Schraal had already darted out the door. Athenor hurriedly stumbled to his feet, knowing there was only one room left where the third skull might be.

He burst into the last room, long-knife still in hand, in time to see Schraal pluck the black *Oculus Velnias* from his pocket and lean toward a central pedestal where the last skull of *Velnias* perched. He felt menace emanate from it, along with a dreadful hunger and anticipation. To one side was a throne seating a dim, motionless shape in the shadows.

Schraal wheeled at his intrusion and lifted his *khukuri* for an overhead swipe. Athenor instinctively dodged the blade that would have sliced into the left side of his neck. He shoved Schraal's arm forward with his left hand, simultaneously slicing the forearm underside with his knife.

Schraal yelped and dropped the *khukuri* from an arm that was suddenly crippled. Uttering a low moan, he swiveled back toward the pedestal, lunging out with his left hand to insert the gem into the waiting skull.

Athenor felt a momentary qualm, remembering his guilt about the many men he had killed. He aimed the point of the scramasax for Schraal's left wrist instead of his heart and neatly skewered it. The pastor's fingers reflexively opened and dropped the gem, which slid across the floor to bump against the skeletal hoofs at the foot of the throne.

Athenor shoved Schraal aside and reached for the gem. The pastor whimpered, both arms rendered useless, and bolted past Athenor and out the door. Athenor heard his footsteps drum down the hall in the direction of the spiral staircase.

His fingers closed tightly over the gem, and he drew a breath. Then, grimly eyeing the skull on the pedestal, he lifted his knife and chopped it down, cleaving the skull into bits that scattered over the floor. For a moment, he thought the remnants of its eyes glowered up at him with bitterness and hatred. Then whatever hellish life inhabited it fled and it was merely a jumble of shattered bones.

Velnias would never live again.

Relieved and knowing what he needed to do next, he stepped back into the hall. The door at the end, the first door, suddenly ruptured open, and the throng of Winter Ghosts spilled out, crowded upon each other, their overlapping whispers like the hiss of vipers.

Athenor hurried up the spiral staircase to the roof. He pounded up the steps to emerge into the cupola. His eyes swept the roof and found Schraal huddled in a hatless heap, moaning with pain and misery, gazing at his two maimed and trembling arms. Seeing the pastor posed no further threat, he sheathed his scramasax knife.

All about them, the rain was being slowly enveloped by a rising mist, while above red creases in the tumbling black clouds widened. Then, he saw above them the mouth of the tornado, slowly rotating like a whirlpool, and within it were flashes of lightning.

The Winter Ghosts poured from the cupola but froze. They saw the lowering tornado and of one accord, retreated into the cupola and down into the house, with eerie wails of fright.

But Athenor felt no fear. He stood in the center of the roof and lifted his hand to that rotating mouth, offering the black jewel. He remembered Cholena's words that it could empower other supernatural creatures besides *Velnias* or *Ördög*…Something *Pèthakhue* must also have known.

"No! You mustn't!" Schraal stumbled to his feet and rushed at Athenor, trying to seize the gem with what remained of his useless hands. But too late.

The *Oculus Velnias* was ripped from Athenor's palm and up into the tornado. The gem's lusterless black changed to gleaming crimson and threw a roseate radiance on the swirling walls of wind. And the cascade of raining mist also turned an unearthly pale red, making the raindrops seem a shower of blood.

"No! You devil!" Schraal screamed up at it, lifting his hands as if to snatch the gem back. "You must pay for what you did to Rosamund! I'll stop you!"

But before he could say anything more, he was plucked off his feet and dragged up into the mouth of the tornado, his clothes and hair wildly flinging. Athenor backed away and saw Schraal rapidly soar up and shrink inside the funnel and heard his screams dwindle, fade, and die.

Not waiting to see more and not trusting to any mercy from *Pèthakhue*, he ran to the edge of the roof and hesitated, gauging the distance to the ground. Behind him, the bellow of the tornado deepened to a harsh, constant cacophony and he turned to see the snout of it touch down onto the stone cupola.

Instantly, the cupola exploded into hundreds of shards. Athenor jumped over the side of the roof, narrowly missing that blast of debris. He landed in a large mud puddle in a tangle of limbs, then scrambled to his feet and stumbled away to the edge of the clearing.

There, he turned and watched as the rest of the roof was savagely torn off by the now-crimson tornado and flung miles away. From inside the lodge, he heard the ghosts all cry out in one fearful scream. Then, the mouth of the tornado dipped down inside, and the screams were muffled. They faintly continued, climbing up into the air, higher and higher, and like Schraal's cry, they faded into silence.

Slowly, the tip of the tornado withdrew from the lodge, taking some rubble with it, along with scattered books, folios, pieces of a desk, and fragments of an ebony throne. These were thrown in all directions to crash down into the waving treetops.

The funnel retracted from within the lodge and for an instant, Athenor thought to see those two blue sparks gazing at him again. Then, the rest of it melted into the clouds and the thundering cataract of its voice ebbed and subsided.

The downpour began to slacken, and the wind died away. Athenor staggered to his feet, slouch hat long gone, the leather ribbon tying his queue vanished, his black hair awry.

The White Lodge was again as he had first seen it.

The crumbling ruins of a rectangular stone foundation amid muddy, puddle-patched ground, with a broken black chimney and the jagged remains of a white rear wall that reared starkly.

Debris was still raining down, fragments of walls and floors, bits of furniture, a thousand fluttering pages of parchment. And a shower of human bones.

Athenor realized these were what remained of the travelers that had once entered the lodge but never left.

There was also a motionless body lying in the mud in front of the ruins amid a jumble of shattered furniture, including what resembled a broken bedframe. He approached warily, drawing his scramasax knife, and inspected it.

It was the corpse of a man, clothes all ripped away — evidently by the tornado. But he had been dead for some time, and given the bluish-white pallor, there was no mystery about the cause of death.

He spotted a marking on one naked arm and peered closely with curiosity. It was the tattoo of an owl.

He shook his head with pity and then scanned his surroundings. Other than this body, he was alone in the clearing.

Or so, he believed.

Hidden in the woods on the other side of the glade, a shadowy, hunched figure regarded him with interest, then gathered its robe and trudged away through the underbrush, heading north.

22. Three Missives

One month later, on a warm June morning, there was a sizeable crowd assembled in front of the Pastorius County Courthouse. Some were workmen with shovels and pickaxes over their shoulders, taking time out from razing the ruined foundation of Town Hall. Once it was leveled and filled in, it would become a memorial park.

Newly promoted Chief Justice Simon Groat, Sheriff Egon Richter, and Mayor Gerben Schreur stood on a low podium in front of a gallows. They blocked out any sight of the two dangling bodies behind them that slowly twirled beneath the platform. They were all saying something to the subdued townsfolk, but their voices were not audible to the three men watching from the rear second-floor balcony of the Sheriff's Office just south.

"The trial didn't take as long as I thought," Athenor remarked somberly.

"You may credit your testimony for that, Seth," Ulysse said. "You were quite convincing, especially in your medical opinion about the cause of Maximilian Lindt's death."

"I don't think the jury needed much urging," Oreste commented. "They were outraged about what Bella and Kitzler plotted against Baldur. I think they were more enraged by Bella's adultery than the fact that she failed in her murder attempt."

"And how is Baldur these days?" Ulysse asked out of politeness – empathy was not his strongest trait.

"He's slowly recovering," Athenor replied. He was still treating him. "I think Johanna's nursing has helped quite a bit. He has not had any further seizures since the poisoning was stopped, but he is still weak and somewhat colicky in his bowel. His emotional state – well, that's a different matter."

"I had to dissuade him from coming to the gallows today, you know," Oreste said. "He still loves Bella…er…loved her. Even forgave her if you can believe that."

"I know." Athenor's lips compressed to a grim line. "She wasn't worthy of that love and didn't return it. But in time, his mind will realize what his heart does not."

They all fell silent for a few moments, while the crowd began to dissipate, although one of the three speakers had evidently not finished.

"I'm surprised, Seth, that you declined the congratulatory banquet Schreur offered you," Oreste said. "It's no mean feat you did, after all. The menace of the Winter Ghosts is ended at last."

Before Athenor could reply, Ulysse squeezed his elbow and smiled. "You don't know our doctor here. He's not one for attention or praise."

Athenor squirmed with embarrassment before replying, "I am grateful that they offered me Kitzler's clinic."

"They had no one else available," Ulysse joked. "Have you accepted? After getting that missive from Dereham?"

Athenor fished in his pocket and withdrew a crumpled letter and looked at it again for the tenth time. When Oreste raised a quizzical eyebrow, Athenor said, "It's from my young apprentice, Stephen Marble. It seems that my rival physician in Dereham, James Tutwiler, has brought in his own apothecary, siphoning away any potential new patients. My old patients will keep coming to my shop for a while – until they need to see a doctor again. The only way to save my practice is for me to return to Dereham immediately."

"But you can't," Ulysse said softly. "Our friend needs you."

"I know." Athenor's face was bleak. "I've reluctantly decided to sell my Dereham practice and do what needs to be done for Rodrigo."

"What of young Marble and that servant you recently employed?"

"Miranda Cranford," Athenor replied. "They'll be welcome to join me here if they wish. But I don't expect Stephen to abandon his invalid mother. So, if the Loreley Town Council can wait, I'll be accepting their offer."

"They'll wait," Oreste said. "In the meantime, those three nurses Kitzler employed can cover the town's medical needs… What are their names? Kellett, Blanchard, and Nathan."

Oh yes, Alistair Nathan. You will soon be looking for a new job. Athenor had not forgotten the nurse's cowardice at Fort Saint Michael in Droitwijk in 1752. "I'll miss some of my old friends in Dereham – Colonel Bernard Reynolds, Malcolm

Ives Herbert Kelly, Donovan Mewes. And I'll miss Dereham, too, my home for the past twelve years."

"I won't miss it," rasped Ulysse. "That thankless mayorship, that worthless Dereham Town Council. They're welcome to have that illiterate idiot Leigh Kynaston as their new judge." He removed a missive of his own and waved it angrily. "I should have expected no less."

"In your case, cousin, I think it's for the best," Oreste smiled at him.

"I suppose so," Ulysse said doubtfully, "in its own dismal little way."

"Cousin, I'm confident that our governor here in Pennsylvania will confirm your appointment to Associate Judge of Pastorius County."

"We'll see," Ulysse turned back to Athenor. "Is there anything else you can tell us about Rodrigo? Who sent the letter? What do you expect you to do – all alone?"

Athenor wrestled with his thoughts. There was only so much he could reveal. He could not tell the full truth – he had only revealed that to Bernard Reynolds and… Rodrigo Archer. His mind returned to the other missive he had recently received, forwarded by Laerte von Mardure in Leichtenberg. It was written in French. What had it said?

It was from his old friend and mentor, Father Joseph Lacouer, from Fort Saint-Germain – the French stronghold on the northeastern shore of Lake Ontar'io. He had been astonished to hear from the Jesuit priest – whom he had not seen for more than twelve years. The letter told him that Lieutenant Archer and his scouting party had been captured by the French and were being held prisoners at the fort. When he went to minister to him, the lieutenant said he knew Athenor and his history and asked him to send a missive. Lacouer was surprised to learn that Athenor was still alive, having long thought of him otherwise.

Lacouer confided in his missive that there was some pressure being placed on the commandant, André de Villemont, to hand him over to some of their Abenaki allies – who claimed Archer and his men had perpetrated atrocities. The priest had no illusions about what those Abenakis would do to Archer and begged him to come and intercede.

Most astonishing of all in what Lacouer wrote was that Athenor was not considered a traitor or deserter, but a hero who had demolished Fort White Pine and who would be welcomed back.

All of that was much to unpack, but there could be no question that Athenor would comply. It was not in his nature to turn his back on a plea for help from anyone, let alone his dearest friend.

But it would mean lies and deceit. He would have to ingratiate himself with his former comrades and commanders in the French Colonial Marines and, either by guile or force, somehow free Archer and his companions and flee back to British America. He might be able to be reinstated in La Marine to further that plan, but what then? To betray and desert them all over again? And what would he do if the situation demanded that he kill his fellow Frenchmen – could he do that to men who trusted him - his own countrymen? And all of this in the middle of the burgeoning war. And as a Marine, could he be required to kill the British and the Provincials who had been of his adopted nation since 1743?

It all made the battle against the Winter Ghosts seem slight by comparison.

His attention was drawn to the gallows below, as the last of the crowd dispersed. The three on the podium had already left. He could see the two hanging bodies with bags covering their heads beneath the scaffold. He watched them as they slowly twirled in their nooses amid the shadows.

He found himself almost envying them.

EPILOGUE

That same morning was also sunny 130 miles to the northeast in New York Province. Mountains of white cloud drifted over the quiet waters of a vast blue lake situated amid green, forested hills. The local Mohawks called it *Onénya' Tkaranto* — "Stone Lake" — because of several small islands that dotted its surface like a handful of strewn pebbles. It was one of the headwaters of the Susquehanough River, of which the Paradise River was a tributary. The surrounding area was inhabited solely by Mohawks, dwelling along its bays and points, but they were hospitable to their Provincial allies, and it was not unusual to see white fishermen there hoping for lake trout or walleye.

Heynrick Rooijakkers was one of them, a Dutch fisher and trapper, a stout man of early middle age. He had just finished fishing for the day, satisfied with the catch stored in his wicker creel, and was trudging through the forest back toward the Mohawk village guesting him.

He walked along the trail in a pleasant haze fueled by a clay jug of rum, fishing pole over his shoulder. He idly noted the chatter of squirrels and the flash of blue jays darting through the trees, crying out their high-pitched jeers.

Those sounds abruptly died and he paused uncertainly, wondering if something had startled them. Surely it could not be any hostile Native this far from any Cayuga or Oneida encampment. Then, by degrees, he became aware that someone was standing in the shadow of an overarching oak.

For a moment, he thought it was another, smaller tree, so motionless it was.

Then, he could pick out details – a man of average height wearing a brown, ankle-length robe and wearing a conical-crowned hat whose broad brim threw his face into shadow. He was leaning with gnarled hands upon a staff with a crook at the end.

"Be not alarmed, friend," a voice said evenly. "I'm merely a priest on a pilgrimage, passing through these parts."

"Well, you gave me a start at that, er…is it – Father?"

"Some have called me that." The man did not move from the shadow of the oak. "But I confess I have lost my way. I haven't traveled around here for many years."

"Where are you bound?" Despite the lack of any ostensible threat, Rooijakkers felt uneasy.

"I used to know a stone house on an island some distance north of here. There was a trading and deer-hunting settlement near it, made up mostly of Dutchmen."

"I'm a Dutchman," Rooijakkers volunteered. "I think I know where you mean – Dereham. But it hasn't been a settlement for many years. It's a full-grown town with more English folk than Dutch."

"As I said, I have been gone for a long time." There was an edge to his voice that Rooijakkers did not like. "But the stone house on the island – in the river nearby. Is it still there?"

"Last I heard of it, Father," the fisherman began cautiously. "But I wouldn't go there if I were you. It's always had a bad reputation, and even worse since last year. It's rumored that it's inhabited by some evil animal-ghosts."

The man did not answer for several moments, then let out a sigh. "I must confess that I don't care for ghosts very much…I believe I've changed my mind."

Rooijakkers could think of no reply, and at length the man silently tipped his hat and started away through the trees, taking another path. His footfalls faded and the sounds of the birds and the squirrels slowly resumed.

Rooijakkers shook his head quizzically, uncertain of what to make of this mysterious priest. He finally shrugged and started on his way. Then, he stopped short and squinted down at the ground at a line of prints that led in the direction the priest had gone.

Surely, he told himself, they must have been there before, made by some deer or perhaps even a goat that had escaped from the Mohawk village. Then he realized — they were not made by something with four feet, but something with two.

Although a tepid churchgoer, he quickly made the sign of the cross and hurried away, looking back over his shoulder, and mumbling a prayer.

For the prints were those of cloven hoofs.

<u>END</u>

AFTERWORD

For many years, I've had recurring dreams about tornados – usually, I'm driving in the countryside beneath a stormy sky when a tornado touches down and begins to pursue me. I will speed off in a different direction only to find a second tornado coming toward me and then divert to find yet another tornado converging on me as if they were all animate beings. So far, they have not caught me. Although I'm an almost-retired psychologist, I've resisted making any interpretation of these dreams, since they provide useful fodder for my writing, and I don't want to "kill the dream" for that reason.

But, as other dreams have with other stories, this one provided the springboard for the current story. Since I was already planning to set an Athenor novel in my fictitious Pastorius County (roughly corresponding to what would one day become Lackawanna County), I decided to combine it with that, after researching to confirm that tornados are not uncommon in that part of the country. Although I'm writing fantasy rather than historical or realistic fiction, I've tried to be faithful to some genuine details in the service of verisimilitude.

In the real world, at the time of this story (1755), this region was inhabited solely by the Lenape; my construct of Loreley Town is completely fictitious, as is the account of its founding by a breakaway group of German settlers once devoted to Franz Pastorius (the real-life founder of Germantown, PA.). Its location was meant to roughly correspond with what would become Scranton (which obviously has a quite different history).

As to the mythological elements, I have borrowed from several sources. *Pèthakhue* and *Maxáxâk* are genuine Lenape myths, indeed a "Thunder-Being" and a "Horned Serpent," respectively, legendary adversaries. However, the Children of the Storm – miniature versions of a tornado – are my invention and are not derived from mythology.

Interestingly, this duality between beings of the air and a serpent monster is replicated in the mythology of other cultures – Scandinavian, Russian, and Slavic. It was from Slavic legendry that I borrowed the underworld demon, *Ördög* or anagrammatically, *Drögö*, who is indeed depicted as a satyr-like creature, human above the waist, but goat-legged and footed below. He is said to be a shapeshifter and sometimes appears as a Hungarian shepherd with glimmering dark eyes. He was normally to be found in Hell, stirring a cauldron filled with the souls of the damned.

Velnias – otherwise called *Veles* or *Volos* – was a male demon in Slavic mythology, said to be the opponent of their chief thunder god *Perun*. He is typically depicted as a dragon or a chimeric bear-snake and was associated with the underworld (as well as with nature, music, wealth, and... cattle!). I've borrowed him as the "Cerberus" for my invented mythology, reassigning his gender in the process. The "Eye of *Velnias*" is my own emendation and does not derive from the original myth.

The Dungeon of the Angels and its reputed history is also my invention. However, it was inspired by the legendary Gates of Hell thought to be in various places of the world –

Central Asia, China, Northern India, Japan, East Africa, and Nicaragua.

And in York County, PA (in the southeastern part of the state).

There are two local legends about the so-called "Seven Gates of Hell" in that vicinity, one relating to a haunted woods and the other to the ruins of an insane asylum. Both asserted that anyone who passed down a road through all seven gates would enter Hell. The name of the road was Toad Road, which reportedly did exist, although destroyed by a hurricane in 1972. When I came across this legend, I already had determined that the terminus of my road would be the entrance to the Dungeon but decided to borrow the name of that defunct road.

The present story paves the way for future stories set in Pastorius County, where Athenor has tentatively agreed to immigrate. His recent lengthy stays in Leichtenberg and now Loreley Town made it too much of a stretch to realistically maintain his apothecarial practice in Dereham, what with him being gone for six months or more. However, whether he returns to accept the Loreley Town Council's offer of taking over Kitzler's practice remains to be seen. After all, the French and Indian War is beginning to start in earnest, which predictably will sweep him up into it.

For the next Athenor novel, I'm not intending to continue the present chronology (i.e. the attempted rescue of Rodrigo Archer in Canada), but instead will return to another prequel:

He has just settled in Dereham after the events in 1743, having joined the medical practice of Dr. Riddle and reconciled himself to an uneasy subordination to Major Staggworth at Fort Silver Crown. But this peace was not to last, for something has started to appear on the North Road, the road skirting the 50-mile length of the eastern edge of the Great Dereham Swamp where several ranches and farms are situated:

A ghostly coach like those seen in England in the 1600s. What spectral occupant broods inside it, no one can say – merely because many travelers who encounter it end up dead or dying, their bodies ravaged and…gnawn.

- Peter Telemark

(08/2023)

www.ingramcontent.com/pod-product-compliance
Lightning Source LLC
Chambersburg PA
CBHW031537150726
47990CB00001B/204